DANCING IN THE WHITE ROOM

Other Books Written As Annie Hoff

Georgette Alden Starts Over

Deslisle Publications

Dancing In The White Room
Wild Snow, I

By

Ute Carbone

CLIMAX, SK
CANADA

Copyright 2019 by Ute Carbone
October 2019
ISBN 978-1-989276-11-2
Cover Art by JE Smith
Produced in Canada

Dedication

To my Dad, who taught me to love skiing.

Acknowledgements

There are a group of writers who have given me support and encouragement through all my writing trials and tribulations and to whom I owe more than I can ever repay. Kate Johnson, Tammy McCracken, Sherry Steffensmeier, Suzanne Ahmad, Fran LeMoine, Tresa Jones, Deborah Jelly, Alex Hayes, Kathy Pyle, Harriet Reindeau, Suzanne Schryrver, and Lana Ayers—thanks for listening and writing and sharing.

Chapter One

The alarm goes off at four-thirty, not that it matters. I'm wide awake and staring at the skylight of our sleeping loft. It's because I had the dream again, the one I keep having over and over since Bell decided he would go back to Alaska, to ski down the West Rib of Denali.

In the dream, I'm standing at the edge of a precipice with Bell. A north wind blows, snow swirls around us. It is so, so cold, my fingertips are frozen. My feet have gone numb. Bell whispers into my ear and tells me it will all be fine. This makes my heart soar and when he kisses me, the warmth from his lips radiates outward to ease the frozen edges of my body. In the logic of dreams, he already has his skis on. I know what he is about to do and I hold onto his gloved hand and beg him no! It will be fine; he repeats and he skis over the edge and disappears into the swirling snow. I'm left holding his empty glove.

He is gone. I can't see him anymore and I know, in my heart and my soul, I know he is gone. I feel his absence in the very marrow of bones, and I wake up with a start—as I always do, my heart pounding as a mix of grief and fear and anger surges through me.

I reach over to make sure he's still there. Living and breathing and with me in this bed in our sleeping loft. Touching his arm, I feel relief. But it lasts no longer than the touch. As I come awake, reality hits me. Tomorrow, if I reach for him he will not be there. Tomorrow, his side of the bed will be empty. Later today, he will be on his way to Alaska. To make his attempt at the West Rib. The descent that nearly killed him the last time he tried. The descent that will send him over the precipice and leave him at the wild, unknown mercy of ice and snow.

Bell bangs on the clock to keep it from singing out again. I turn my back to him and nestle under the blankets. It's not only in dreams that it is cold. It's late February and it shouldn't be as cold as it is—it was five below when I checked the thermometer propped outside the kitchen window last night. The temperature inside does not seem much warmer. Bell would probably say I'm the one causing the freeze. We've spent the past few days fighting. I've done my share of pleading and cursing. I refused to help him pack his gear.

Bell's hand comes to my waist soon enough. His long fingers caress my side and follow up under the curve of my breast.

"Mallory, you awake?"

I try to decide if I should answer him. I try to decide whether I want to have this conversation again, the one we've had off and on for the last six months, ever since he let slip he would be going back to Alaska.

I've never been good at pretense, so I turn to face him. His face is angular in the gray light of the room, his blond hair shuffles around his shoulders. He reaches over, his arm still warm from the down of our comforter and kisses the arch of my shoulder.

"I'm going to miss that." His voice is as inviting as a warm bath in the winter surrounding our cabin.

It would be easy to fall into his warmth, easy to make this goodbye tender and inviting, the way our goodbyes usually are. Soft and intense, full of a kind of sweetness that can hold us, both of us, for a week or a month. A goodbye that promises a return, that says we'll be here again, together.

Today, I push him away. I'm in no mood for sweet goodbyes. Last minute lovemaking won't change his mind. And what I want is a mind change. What I want is a turnaround. I'm too scared to settle for less.

"Jesus, Mallory," Bell says before turning his back to sit up on the bed. In the dim light, I can see the outline of the mountain tattooed on his shoulder. Denali, a view of Wickersham's wall on the north face, a reminder of the first time he challenged this mountain, the highest on the continent. That time he challenged it and won. That first time he came home to me.

He gets up, his body a spring. Sleek and long, graceful. He moves as though he is made of pure energy. He throws his clothes on, throws a few last-minute items into his beat-up EMS pack, and looks back at me. In this light I can't see his face clearly, but I know what his eyes are saying anyway. He pauses, puts the pack down, and climbs back onto the bed and pulls me back into him. He smells of soap and wood smoke. I can almost taste him and I feel my body start to soften. I won't give in to it. I break away from his embrace.

"Don't leave it like this," he says, an unvoiced please fluttering at the end of the sentence. A white flag, but not surrender.

"You're the one who's decided on this suicide mission." I wish I were fully dressed so it would be easier to take a stand.

He's losing patience. "Six weeks. I'll be back in six weeks. Please quit being so fucking melodramatic."

This is the wrong approach. I turn on my side and bury myself in the blankets. I half hope he'll think it over again. He'll change his mind. He'll stay.

I hear him pick up his pack, hear his footsteps on the stairs. It's all I can do not to follow. In a few minutes, after the door slams shut and the Jeep's gravely report from the driveway's done, I'll allow myself a good hysterical fit. Then I'll pick myself up and get on with the day.

I hear our dog, Chance, scraping across the floor and bounding down the stairs. Chance isn't troubled by pride. I can picture Bell; bent on one knee to give Chancie's ears a scratch. I close my eyes against the picture.

Bell's voice floats up the stairs, calmer than I expected, soft really, tinged with just enough sad to make me want to cover my ears. "Hey, munchkin," he says. "What are you doing up?"

It's not the dog he's talking to, but our four-year-old daughter, Emily. I can picture her, too, a miniature version of her father. Same wild blonde hair, same intensity in her blue eyes. I imagine she's rubbing them now, clearing away the dreams she's had, and she's wandered out from her room to see her daddy. He's right up there with Santa and the Easter Bunny when it comes to her outright unrestricted love of the man. I imagine she's giving him a hug. I can't quite make out the tired little voice, but she's telling him something.

"I've got to go, sweetie," I hear Bell tell her. "Take care of Mommy for me, okay?"

Now I don't have to wait for tears. They're floating to my eyes unbidden. I'm up and in my robe and ready to fly down the stairs, but I hear the front door shut, and then my little girl's on the stairs, coming up to me.

She sits on the bed, her eyes soft in the semi-dark. "Mommy, are you crying?"

"A little," I say, because there's no sense in being dishonest with Emily Bell. She'd ferret out the lie a mile away. She puts her hand to my knee, a small breadth of fingers.

"Don't worry," she says. "It'll be okay."

I gather her up and give her a tight squeeze she soon wriggles out of. I hope she's right. I hope it will be okay. That somehow, life will be the way it was before.

She watches me, a little wary. She won't put up with my tears for too long.

"How about breakfast?" I say, as I hear Bell's Jeep pull out of the drive.

My friend Creech calls at seven. I'd coaxed Emily back to sleep in my bed after placating her with a toaster waffle and had finally drifted off myself. My voice must sound a little groggy because Creech asks if he woke me. I tell him I had to get up anyway.

"Can you give me a ride to the hill? The clutch on my truck's popped again."

"Sure, what's in it for me?"

"I'll make coffee."

"And?"

"And nothing, Prescott. Coffee's my final offer."

Creech doesn't mention Bell, although he knows today's the day he leaves for Alaska. He knows it's a sore spot with me. In most matters, Creech is Switzerland. He likes to stand on neutral ground.

I get Emily up and dressed for the day. Our ski stuff is already packed in the back of my Cherokee, which is sitting just shy of the detached garage. The garage is full of ski and climbing equipment and Bell's workbench, too full to actually house either one of our vehicles. Emily's grumbling. She's a good sleeper and the early morning interruption doesn't sit well with her. I make her another waffle, throw some toast in for me and try to decide if it's warm enough to put Chance on the lead outside. It's warmed some. The thermometer says it's up to ten degrees, and Chance is whining and pawing at the door, so I decide to put him out.

"Won't he be cold, Mommy?" my little girl asks.

"He's got a thick coat. He's made for cold weather." Chance is a malamute, a gift from Bell's climbing partner, Roddie Kirchman. "A little taste of Alaska," as Rod put it, and the dog loves nothing better than snow. In this way, I guess he's a lot like Bell and me. Snow gets to be a habit living in North Elba, just outside Lake Placid, in five acres of pinewood surrounded by the well-rounded bald heads of the McIntyre Range. It's not such a bad habit to keep.

We finally get it all settled. Chance is on the chain by his doghouse. He rolls around in the snow. The chain is long enough to give him free range of the yard, though the tether doesn't satisfy him. Twice, he's broken free. When Bell comes home, we'll fence the yard or maybe get one of those invisible dog fences.

If Bell gets home.

The thought skitters through my brain again. I

16

chase it away. I've been with Bell for seven years, long enough to know worrying over him will only serve to drive me crazy. Skiing down big mountains is what he does. The bigger the vertical drop, the more difficult, the more Bell wants to conquer it. He loves to push the envelope, craves the excitement of skiing on the edge. Craves it like a user craves drugs.

I've always thought I understood his need for challenge. I fell in love with him, at least in part, because he was untamed, as wild and free as the mountains surrounding us. I loved him all the more for being fearless. But my mind keeps flipping back to last time. He's tried this descent before, and last time? It nearly killed him Which nearly did me in, too.

I can still hear Rod Kirchman's voice, his Crocodile Dundee accent crackling over the satellite phone. "There's been an accident. Bell's taken a fall."

Those words turned my knees to water, made my heart plummet like a runaway elevator shaft. It felt as though I'd been the one to take the fall, as though I were the one who needed to be air-vaced to the nearest hospital.

It might have been easier if it had been me. Sustaining three fractured ribs, two broken legs, a busted collarbone and a concussion would have hurt much less than seeing someone I love in that condition.

Bell would tell me later he'd been lucky. He'd stopped just a few feet short of a precipice. A few feet and good luck—the only separation between life and death.

Time has passed since then. We have a daughter now. Before she was born, he promised me he wouldn't try that particular descent again. It's a promise he decided not to keep.

It's not that I don't understand his love of skiing. I was practically born with skis attached to my feet. My dad and Creech's folks own a small ski area an hour and change south of here. Creech and I grew up on the hill. We both ski still. He coaches J-II girls, young Olympic hopefuls, and I'm on the patrol staff at Whiteface. I can't argue for Bell to give up skiing when giving it up is something I could never do myself.

Emily and I are out the door by seven-thirty. Bell's down in Albany by now, boarding a plane to Chicago, the first leg of a long trek. Today he'll reach as far as Anchorage, some three thousand miles from our home here in the Adirondacks. I can picture him, boarding pass at the ready, pack slung over his shoulder. I wonder if he's remembered to eat breakfast, or, if caught up in what he's doing, he's forgotten to eat all together.

I drive down River Road towards route 83 and Whiteface Mountain. Creech lives just off this road a few miles down from the cabin, in an old farmhouse that he bought last fall and hopes to renovate with Bell's help once the ski season's done.

I haven't seen Creech in a while. He's been busy with the Junior Olympics that were recently concluded on the hill. He'd quit shaving, a kind of good-luck thing to give the girls an edge. I asked if he'd quit changing his underwear too, and he said that he would, if he thought it would help.

I pull into the drive, honk twice, and there's Creech on the saggy front porch, shouldering a huge gear bag, coffee-less and beard-less.

He stows his bag next to mine and Emily's, says "Hey, munchkin" to my daughter, and climbs into the seat next to me. It's a bit of a shock to see him clean shaven again. He looks more like the kid he used to be, back when we were growing up in Wells.

"Where's my coffee?" I ask as I pull out of the drive.

"Ran out of time. Got busy shaving."

"Must have taken you a while."

When he smiles, a little dimple forms in the corner of his mouth, and his green eyes, flecked with tiny specks of gold, light up. Creech and I dated all through high school, and I know how appealing those eyes can be. Since then, he's been busy trying to date every available woman who's ever set foot on, or near, a ski area. He has two rules. The women have to be at least twenty-one (this because half the girls he coaches have a severe crush on him), and they can't live within an hour of his house. He's serious about these criteria and never allows himself to break his own rules.

"I'll buy you a coffee on the hill." He's watching me and I know he's thinking about Bell, though he doesn't say anything and I'm not about to bring it up. Creech is no stranger to skiing and risk. He used to be a downhill racer, a good one on the FIS circuit. He skied with the US team for a few years, and would have gone to the Olympics, if he hadn't taken a really nasty fall during a training run in Grindlewald. He shattered both knees, missed the Olympic trials, and spent the next season trying to get back his standing. But he lost his edge. There's a narrow line that separates first place from thirtieth, and it became impossible to cross. Seven years ago, he came to Lake Placid as a coach and he's been here ever since.

The year Creech moved to Lake Placid, I graduated college. I moved to Albany and got a soul-sucking job working in a cube farm for the state of New York. I had a studio apartment and a boyfriend named Tommy. Tommy asked me to marry him about every other week.

My parents had gone through a painful divorce when I was in high school, and my mom never tired of telling me what an awful husband my dad had been. I was my father's daughter, so much like him I figured saying 'I do' wouldn't work for me either.

So I put Tommy off, told him not yet. Said I'd think about it. Then Creech called and invited me up to his new digs in Lake Placid for the weekend.

"You can't be serious," Tommy said when I told him.

"You can come too," I said, thinking that would ease his mind.

"Why would I want to spend the weekend holed up in some crappy apartment with your ex-boyfriend?" he shot back.

"Suit yourself," I said.

He took it to mean 'go fuck yourself.' Maybe I did mean that, because things hadn't been good between us and I'd gotten to where I didn't care what he thought. I packed my overnight bag and left early the next morning.

On the Northway, out past the cities and the suburbs and the malls and the traffic, the cotton I had been breathing became the clear still air of Route 73. I could name the sights: Cathedral Rocks, Giant Falls, the two long elliptical Cascade Lakes. All of them looked as though they had been waiting for me, inviting me north and hoping that I would stay a while.

It started raining when I reached Lake Placid, a cold November rain that turned to snow and splattered onto the windshield in quick-melt flakes. A fog hung dense and low over Mirror Lake. It was to rain the whole weekend. And I was to be about as happy as I'd been anywhere in my twenty-two years of life.

Creech took me up to Whiteface that Saturday. We took a six-pack and sloshed through ankle-deep mud to the base of one of the chairlifts. The chairs were lined on a cable that disappeared into the mist as it threaded up the hill. The rocks shimmered under the dripping towers. We sat in a chair under cover, the pulley just over our heads, opened two Millers, and toasted Creech's good fortune. We laughed and talked and drank, and when it came time to leave, a sadness crept over me like the fog, damp and wet and heavy.

I must have shown what I was feeling because Creech asked me what was wrong. I shrugged. "I have to go home tomorrow. I'm going to miss this place. I miss it already."

Creech took a last swig from the beer can. "You're crazy, you know," he said.

"No, I'm not. I'm just doing what's expected with my life. There's nothing wrong with working in an office and living in the city with Tommy."

Creech said, "Skiing's in your blood, Mallo. You can't keep denying it."

His words followed me all the way back down Route 73 the next day. By the time I got to the end of the Northway, I'd made up my mind. Creech was right. I was crazy.

A month later, I quit my job, quit Tommy, packed all my stuff into the back of my Fiesta, and took off for the north into what I hoped was not the train wreck my mom predicted.

Chapter Two

It hasn't been a train wreck. A wild ride maybe, I think as I drive up the access road to Whiteface, but not a train wreck.

The early arrivals are already finding their way to the lodge, skis and boards hung over shoulders, bags clanking against hips. Kids struggle under the weight of their equipment, wrapped up tight in jackets and hats and gloves with nothing showing but their eyes. Equipment is stacked teepee-style against posts. People line up for lift tickets. And I get to be here, nearly every day, all winter long.

I tell Creech he still owes me coffee.

He trails off with his stuff. "What about lunch?"

"Will I have to buy?" I tease. Creech and I have a long-standing challenge over whose turn it is to pick up the check.

He cocks his head and smiles. "Don't think it's my turn."

This is my life. This is the way it should be. I trail my own stuff to the post outside the aid station, and then bring Emily to the nursery to leave her with Charlotte, the soft-spoken blonde who runs the onsite daycare. Emily's one of the only regulars here, and she walks in like she owns the place. I tell her I'll see her at lunch.

This is my life, the one I've been living happily-ever-after for the last seven years. Perfect, if only. And here it comes, the if only. If only P.D. Bell would quit chasing descents down mountains

23

perilous enough to challenge him, which means perilous enough to kill him.

In the aid station, there's a map of the area stuck with pushpins. Each pin represents the scene of an accident, some mishap we've had to respond to. The bottom of the hill, where the slope is flatter, easier, and well-groomed, is littered with pins. Most all accidents happen here—some due to inexperience, some to lack of caution. Most accidents are relatively minor—a sprained ankle, a turned knee, a separated shoulder. The top of the hill where the steeps are, the expert trails marked with two black diamonds, the "off trail" trails of slides and glades that the groomers don't reach, has very few pins. It takes concentration to ski that terrain; the vertical requires you pay attention. In fact, I can name only two off-trail accidents on the steeps. Two years ago, a ski patrolman named Sully Sullivan took a dixie off the slide and fractured both legs. And five years ago, Johnny Ahern, a champion bumps skier, lost control and had a head-on collision with a tree in the glades. He died on his way to the hospital. Albie Albertson, the head of patrol, uses the map as an illustration to rookie patrollers. They don't fall often in the steeps, he'll tell them, but when they do they fall hard.

Albie's been head of patrol going on forever, and if you ask him exactly how long it's been, he'll point to the mass of gray hair on his head and say "a very long time." Albie's washed blue eyes are scanning the aid room, and they fall on me as I come in late. I apologize. It's the first time this season I have been late, but still, it embarrasses me. And the fact that everyone in the room knows about Bell's leaving makes me even more uncomfortable. I make a silent promise I won't let it happen again.

I partner with Coyote Mathers for morning sweep. We take the Cloudsplitter Gondola up to Little Whiteface Peak and make our way down Cloudsplitter glades to Upper Empire. We do this every morning, making sure the terrain is skiable and marking off any rough patches. The glades hang off the side of the mountain, a series of bushwhack trails thick with trees. It's bush without the whack, Bell would say. The groomers are kept off, so those who ski or board well enough can have an adventure. Unlike Bell's adventures, the base lodge is nearby and there's first aid available, if it's needed.

I can see the glades from my perch on the gondola. They are impacted and blistered with ice. Rocks erupt like a bad case of acne. The snow that does exist whispers close to the trees, and though I can't see this from here, I know it's crud, snow that has frozen and refrozen. Snowmaking has kept the hill open, and most of us would be happy with a good snowstorm to improve things.

Coyote and I pick our way through the rutted passages under the trees. It's icy and my skis skid over the surface.

"This is some shitty shit," says Coyote.

"You're right. The passes aren't safe. We'll have to rope them off."

Upper Empire is in much better shape, though the moguls are glazed over. A cold wind scurries out through the trees and catches us as we ski through.

"Is it ever going to warm up?" I mutter.

"Buck up, Mallo. Spring's just around the corner." Unfortunately, Coyote doesn't look like he means it.

It's Saturday and the local schools are on winter break, which means the slopes are crowded. We're kept pretty busy and before I know it, it's lunchtime. I pick up Emily and we go to the base lodge to find Creech already halfway through a bowl of chili. I get lunch for Emily and me and ride him for not buying. He calls me a mooch, but he goes off and gets coffee for us and hot chocolate for Emily and then says we can call it even.

Corky Peters joins us as I crumble crackers into Emily's chicken noodle soup and then blow on it because she says it's too hot. Corky's one of the first people I met when I settled in Lake Placid.

I came with my wagonload of stuff and crashed on Creech's couch for a week. I knew I wanted to work on the hill, so the first thing I did was go see Albie Albertson. Though he couldn't offer me a fulltime job, he was impressed with my background. I'd gone to school at Middlebury on a ski scholarship, broken a couple of racing records. And my dad owned a ski area. He took me on part-time, with the understanding that if I passed EMT training and the ski patrol certification tests given in Vermont in February, I could work full time on paid staff the following season. I was thrilled. The part-time job didn't pay more than free lift tickets, which was something I was looking for at the time. But free lift tickets wouldn't pay rent and groceries. So the second thing that I did after arriving in Lake Placid was to look for a job.

I applied for, and got, a waitress job advertised in the local community paper. It was at a tiny place called the Benchmark, which was owned by the chef, a guy named Leo Jenkins, a transplant from Manhattan.

Corky taught me everything I know about

waiting tables. Without her, I'm pretty sure Leo would have fired me during my first few weeks at the Benchmark.

Creech says he has to go back to work and reminds me I need to give him a ride home. He is not Corky's biggest fan. They both spend a lot of time dating people from out of town. Somehow, Creech holds this against her, though I don't see how it's a fault in her and not in him.

Corky shakes her head at him, though she doesn't say anything about his hasty departure, and I don't want to go there myself. She hammers instead right into other unspoken territory. "So how you doing Bell-less?" she asks.

I don't answer her. She's been a friend for a while, and I'm grateful for those early days, but we don't spin in the same circles anymore. And I know that she thinks Bell is some sort of Norse God who is yet again proving his immortality. I really don't want to get into it. Luckily, I don't have to because Emily's squirming in her seat, asking if I'll take her to the summit.

I checked the thermometer right before I left the first aid station. It was up to a balmy twenty degrees. I'm thankful for the jump up, although the wind's still strong enough to make the chairlifts bob and there's ice aplenty on top. Emily has not yet been to the summit, and she spends most days making her plea. Her best argument is that her daddy would take her. And it's true, if Bell hadn't been caught up in training, he would have taken our little girl out. But I'm not willing to risk it, not today. Emily pouts at me and I'm about to tell her we won't go out at all.

Corky says, "Hey, baby Bell, I want to see your stuff. What you say we get Mom here to take us up

27

the quad?" The quad chair goes halfway up the summit, serving a bunch of intermediate trails. Emily's done these before, and I'm comfortable with the compromise.

Emily's excited. She likes the idea of showing off her stuff. I tell her we need to get her helmet, and she's not so happy anymore.

"If you're going to ski the big hill, you have to protect your head."

"Mom," she says in a way that makes me think she's already a teenager.

"Daddy and I both agree on this, Em."

"Fine." She shrugs as if it's no big deal.

I leave her with Corky while I run down to the ski shop to pick up the helmet I ordered for her last week.

Marty Callahan and Turk Millet are down in the shop. It's quiet now that most of the rentals have been meted out. I groan inwardly at the sight of Turk, a rookie patrol guy who's made some comments about my ass, thinking I might take them as compliments. I paste on a smile and walk in. Right above where the boys sit, there's a poster of Bell jumping Hole in the Wall at Crystal in Washington State. In it, he's flying over a pile of rocks. It's a spectacular shot, blue-brushed sky, Bell's blond hair ribboned behind him, his skis floating in air supernaturally. Looking at it, you can see where Corky might think he's more god than human. I guess there was a time when I thought so myself too.

Bell was, and still is, legendary around here. I met him in March of my first year on patrol, just as the snow was melting into puddles on Main Street in Lake Placid. He was on the X-games circuit then, and a couple of the extreme skiers and boarders were coming out to Whiteface to stage a demo. P.D. Bell was at the top of the list. He was a local kid, and his biography was something out of a storybook. Raised by his aged grandfather in a cabin in the woods near Saranac Lake, Peter Daniel Bell grew up to be one of the best skiers in the world. By the time he blew into Placid the year we met, he had won six gold medals in X-game and freestyle competition, appeared in three Warren Miller films, done stunts for one Hollywood action movie, had his face smeared across every ski magazine cover, and posed for a ton of ads and posters like the one I was staring at now.

Marty catches me staring at the poster of Bell and smirks at Turk. I pull my eyes away and get down to business. Marty says he'll check to see about the helmet and leaves me alone with Turk.

"Mallicious, what's the matter? Your head not hard enough?" Turk asks.

From other quarters this might be easily ignored. From Turk, it's annoying. I'm senior to him, but he doesn't seem to understand this on account of my having breasts.

"How are the potato peels?" I say, giving him my sweetest girl smile. Turk got poured into the dumpster last week. It's a ritual around here, all the rookies get stuffed into the dumpster or hung up on the chair or find mayonnaise in their gear bags. It's kind of a rite of passage. I got stuffed into the dumpster myself the first month I was here. I smelled like ketchup for a week, but I didn't mind. It meant that they thought I was one of them. A little sister in the big boy operation. Only I've become a big sister now, and Turk is like the brat brother I'd rather not have. He didn't appreciate the dumpster dunk, which is, of course, why I bring it up.

"Nice red diamond on your ass there, Mallo. How's the whole black widow thing working out for you?"

Turk's comeback hits way too close to home and I have to stop myself from popping him, which would be a dumb move on my part as he's a foot taller and at least fifty pounds heavier.

"Since you'll never get that close, it's nothing I'd worry about if I were you," I say. I pay Marty for the merchandise and leave before further comment can be made.

Emily doesn't want to wear the helmet. She complains that it's too tight, which it isn't. I tell her that she'll look cool and remind her that all of Creech's racers wear them.

"I hate it," she says.

It's getting late and we'll have to hurry if we want to get the run in. I play the mother card instead.

"Wear it," I tell her, "because I said so, and I won't take you if you don't."

Emily's eyes narrow and she shoves the helmet onto her head. She says she hopes I'm happy.

It's windy at the top of the lift. The slopes are crowded with skiers traversing down. Emily points to the steepest of the blue square trails and asks if we can do that one. She's only done it once before, but she managed all right, so I buckle her helmet, check her boots and bindings and tell her to go for it. She sails straight down, her legs wedged into a pie, her hands on her knees because she doesn't use poles. At the flat just over the first rise, she executes two graceful turns, swooping past a couple struggling to get down. They both stop to watch her.

30

"Look at the little shit go," says Corky, and I smile, feeling pretty proud. I swoop down the side in a fall line that ought to beat my daughter to the bottom. The snow is crusted and corny, but the bumps on this slope have been groomed out and there's enough loose grain to make the descent an easy and mindless one. I glide down; Albie's warning about carelessness needling its way into my thoughts. I remind myself that the only time I ever took a spill that amounted to a trip to the emergency room was when I was fourteen. I broke my arm on the flats. Creech and I had been messing around, skiing 360s in front of one another. Emily is a red speck at the bottom of the hill, which she's negotiating with ease. On the next snowfall bright day I'll have to take her for a summit run.

Emily stops near the bottom. I swoop in behind her and pick her up. She giggles. She loves this trick. Corky's about halfway down, her blue jacket staining the trees as she weaves back and forth.

"Can we do it again?" Emily asks.

"Nope. I've got to get back to work and you need to go back to school."

"School is boring. They only let us on the little hill."

"Practice makes perfect. You want a ride?"

She jumps up and down on her skis. "Yes, yes, yes!"

"Take my poles then." I hoist her onto my back, piggyback style, one Emily-sized ski flopping down each side and we scoot down towards the lodge. We pass Coyote on the way. He whistles at us. Emily waves at him. And everything is right with my world, at least for a little while.

Chapter Three

I drive Creech up to the auto repair place after work. I swear he should own it by now, considering all the money he gives them to fix his truck. I tell him he ought to get a new vehicle, but he begs off by saying he can't afford it. The truth is he loves that old truck. It's the same one that got him here seven years ago, and he's not ready to part company with it.

Emily goes outside with Chance when we get home. I fry up a couple of burgers and watch her from the kitchen window. She and the dog chase each other through the yard, then Emily climbs up on her swing set. It's only a short reach to the lower branch of a huge maple that stands in our yard. She grabs the branch and swings on that, Chance yapping at her heels. I hold my breath a second. A few times she's climbed up into the tree. Both Bell and I have told her not to, but she's fearless like her father. Each time I try to stay very calm and tell her to come on down. She can't understand what the fuss is about.

"It's nice up there, Mom," she says. Today, she jumps back off the branch and runs inside, and I put my worries aside.

I feed Chance and while he's eating, we sit down with the burgers. Emily nearly falls asleep in hers. For all her complaints about 'school', she comes home happy and tired at the end of the day. I decide to save her bath for morning, and she barely stays awake long enough to put on pajamas.

I clean the dishes once Emily's asleep and can't help but think burgers are Bell's favorite. He says it's because that was what he was eating when he met me, though I don't buy it. I am surprised, though, that he remembers what he was eating when he met me. I remember too.

I saw Bell for the first time while he was skiing with some of his X-games teammates, and the sight is one I can still conjure. His long, lean body flying over moguls, his shadow rushing after him. The first time, it took my breath away.

It was late by the time I got to lunch that day. The demo on the hill had caused an explosion of people and, although it was already well into March, you would have thought it was Christmas week judging by the crowds. We were busy: two sprains, a fractured fibula, and any number of minor emergencies.

Albie had started muttering about the X-team guys. "We should post a warning," he said. "Every Tom, Dick, and Sally suddenly thinks they're PD Bell."

The lunch crowd had long since filtered out of the cafeteria, choosing to stand in line for the lifts rather than hamburgers. I spooned up a bowl of chili from what looked like the dregs of the pot. Bell sat at a corner table with some other guys from the team, his blond hair curled around his shoulders. He was the best-looking guy I had ever laid eyes on. I sat down a few tables down from him. When I looked up, I saw Bell watching me. I smiled and he smiled back, said something to his friends, picked up his tray and started walking in my direction. I figured he was done with lunch and about to leave. I wanted to gaze at him, but not stare, so I concentrated on my chili.

I didn't look up again until he sat down across from me, at which point I was caught up in a kind of gummy, adolescent speechlessness. He had a half-eaten burger on his tray and a mound of fries slathered in ketchup.

"Chili any good?" he asked.

I examined the chili as though it might give me an answer to his question. The crackers I'd been crumbling into the bowl were stuck to my palm. "I wouldn't recommend it." I brushed the crumbs from my hand.

"I was watching you ski," he said. "You're pretty phenomenal." He smiled down at his burger.

"You're not so bad yourself," I answered, thinking the minute after I said it that this was possibly the stupidest thing that had ever dropped out of my mouth.

"You want to grab a beer or something later?"

I had a hard time concentrating for the balance of the afternoon. I kept playing the scene with Bell over in my head. I would play it cool, I decided. I'd have a few beers with him and that would be great. Then we'd go our separate ways.

We met at Carducci's, a little pizza-bar up in Wilmington Notch where everybody hangs out after the lifts close. It was stuffed to the rafters with people. Bell and I had to stand until a table opened. When one finally did, it was a small one and we were pinned near the wall in two chairs opposite one another. People came over to introduce themselves or have me introduce them to Bell. Corky was there, and she joined us at the table. Other people from the mountain, some I knew and some Bell knew from growing up here came over and sat awhile. Bell took it all in stride. He was friendly and smiled a lot, but there was something in the way he kept shifting in his chair, something in the way he kept looking at me that let me know he wasn't comfortable with the notoriety.

The bar was noisy and it was hard to hear. An hour passed and we hadn't said more than a few words to each other. Finally, Bell leaned over the table and asked if maybe I'd like to go somewhere else.

We drove in his rented SUV down Route 86 towards Lake Placid. He didn't say much, but a few miles from Carducci's he pulled into a small lot at the trailhead for Copperas Pond. He sighed, smiled at me, and asked if I wanted to go for a walk.

It was dark by then, with a crescent moon peeking out from behind bare tree branches. The snow was hard and crunchy underfoot. The thought crossed my mind that I must be crazy to follow some guy I hardly knew into the woods at night. But follow I did. We tramped in to the shore of a small pond. There was a rock, a big flat boulder, half dipped into the shallow water, shadowed by the birches and hemlocks. Bell climbed onto the boulder and gave me a hand up. Moonlight scattered across the pond. Bell leaned back on his elbows and stretched his long legs. Above us, a wide berth of stars spread over the deep night sky. Bell held his hand out and pointed. "See that," he said. "That's Orion. And over there is Ursa Major." He stopped pointing and we both sank back to look at the sky. I was aware of the breathing forest all around me and the breath of this man next to me.

"You know a lot about stars," I said.

"Danny, my grandfather, taught me," he said.

We fell into another comfortable silence. I could have stayed there all night, though it was getting a little cold, and Bell said that he ought to take me some place warmer.

"I've never had a date in the forest before," I told him.

"You know what they say," he said. "You can take the boy out of the forest..."

"But you can't take the forest out of the boy," I finished for him. He laughed and reached over and stroked my hair.

"Would it be okay if I kiss you now?"

"I thought you'd never ask."

His mouth was soft and warm, refuge from the cold winter night. The kiss went on for a long time, and I thought if I could sit on that rock forever kissing Bell, my life would be just about perfect.

"Still up for pizza?" he asked once we finally stopped to catch our breath. It was late by then, too late to go back to Carducci's.

"There's a take-out place in town that's open all night. We can go there and bring it back to my place."

His eyes had a curious look in them. "You sure?"

"Yes." I'd never been surer of anything in my whole life.

My place was a tiny one room with a bath. A stove and a refrigerator stood off in one corner pretending to be a kitchen. The rest consisted of a bed and a dresser. We sat on the bed and fed each other pizza. Soon the box was shoved onto the floor along with our clothes, all heaped together in a pile. Bell's hands explored the hollow of my neck, the cleft between my breasts. It felt as though his hands belonged there, as though I had been waiting for him. As though I had always known the curve of muscles along his back, his narrow waist, his long legs tangling with mine. And when his hands moved down over my belly and farther down along to stroke my thighs and the soft cleft between them, it was as though I'd found something I hadn't known I was looking for.

"You're perfect," he whispered, mirroring my thoughts.

That was on Sunday. Bell was in town until Thursday. We spent pretty much every moment between those days together, both in bed and out. I told Bell all about my life, my job. He talked about the freestyle circuit, how he'd been on it for six years now, how it had become a grind. He talked about his love of mountains, and his love for these mountains in particular, the ones he'd grown up in.

He took me to meet his grandfather. Danny still likes to recount the story of the day he met me. "I'd heard it told that PD had his share of pretty girls," he likes to say when reminiscing, "but you're the only one he ever brought home." He lived, still does, way off in the woods in a cabin near Saranac Lake. It was cold the day I met him and he suggested we go out for a stroll. We tacked on snowshoes and headed out into the woods behind the house. There are no trails there, but Danny had spent well over eighty winters in these hills, and they were to him as familiar as his kitchen. Bell had lived there a long time, too. Didn't matter that I didn't know my way through these woods. Danny did, and Bell did. I had the strangest feeling I would too in time.

"Take care of her, PD," Danny said before we left. "This girl's a keeper."

Bell had smiled then. "I know it."

Still, despite all this, I told myself it was only a fling. Bell would be gone come Thursday. And I kept hoping Thursday would never come.

The phone rings as I start up the stairs for bed. It's my mother, who still calls weekly after seven years to ask if I've finally come to senses and am ready to give up this crazy life I've decided on and move back to Albany where it's safe.

Tonight she asks after Bell. She knows he's gone and the fact that she remembers this and that she sides with me puts me in the awkward position of having to defend him.

"I know you love him," she says, "but I'm not sure that's enough."

I don't answer her, so she changes the subject. I guess I have to give her some credit for that.

"You'll never guess who I ran into at the mall today," she says. I don't feel much like guessing and she's never been good at waiting anyway. "Tommy Nussman," She says his name like this is the best news she could give me.

My Tommy? I almost blurt out. I catch myself just in time. He's hardly mine anymore, and he probably never was mine to begin with. I pull a stray sock, covered in dust, out from under the couch. It's one of Bell's, a white one without a match and the singleness of it makes me want to weep.

"He's married, you know," my mother says. "His wife's name is Marla. They're expecting. I showed him a picture of our Emily."

To my mother it is always 'our Emily', though I'm not sure she includes Bell in the 'our'. The comment about Tommy being married is meant to rankle. On another day, she would have asked, and none too discreetly, why Bell and I don't get married. Our not being legally bound is a sticking point with her, especially in light of Emily, and one

38

more reason for her not to like Bell. In my mother's eyes, it's his fault we're not married. Bell's not the marrying kind, she says. He's a lot like my father, she says, who, in her opinion, never should have married. Of course, that would mean I wouldn't be here for Mom to harass, nor Emily either, for that matter, but I guess that didn't figure into the equation.

Thankfully, our conversation takes a different route. Still, after I hang up I'm left with the old nagging questions of my relationship with Bell. I peel them like crumbs from the floor. Does Bell love me? Is he in it for the duration? Questions that have nagged at me ever since Bell breezed into my life seven years ago. And then breezed out of it again. Because that Thursday, seven years ago, came after all.

On that Thursday morning I woke up in my apartment with Bell's body spooned around mine and I told myself the fling was over. I'd had my little romance, and in a few hours Bell would be driving to Albany where he'd catch a plane to Calgary. I braced myself for the inevitable. I was a pit stop in Bell's life. By tomorrow, he'd have forgotten me. By tomorrow, I'd be back to my old new life, waiting tables, skiing, living in my attic apartment. I told myself the fling had been great and I would have no regrets. But when I watched him, his arm pillowed under his head, the sheet all twisted around him, my heart felt caught in a wringer and I knew I was fooling myself.

Still, I kept it light. While he packed, I chatted at him about the end of ski season, about next season (I'd passed certification and would patrol full time next year), about how I'd been to the Canadian Rockies once and the skiing there had been fantastic.

Bell turned and put his arms to my shoulders. "Come with me then," he said. I passed this off. Bell didn't have a home, he had an address in Squaw Valley, a place he kept with a couple of friends. He was footloose. He didn't need me hanging him up.

"I can't," I said. "I promised Leo I'd stay to work the summer, and then there's Albie."

"Oh," said Bell, and maybe it was just conjecture, but I would have sworn he sounded disappointed. A lot disappointed, in fact. His eyes misted over when he kissed me goodbye. "I'll come back then," he said.

Chapter Four

The year I met Bell, we closed the ski area in mid-April, after a big spring fling extravaganza only the die-hards and the locals attended. It had been a month since Bell left, and I hadn't heard from him. I didn't know it then, but this would be the predicate on which our relationship was set. Bell would go off for a week or a month, and then he'd come back. So far he's always come back. Though that first time it took him a long while.

I had no expectations. I figured on forgetting him and it shouldn't have been hard to do. His name would pop up now and again on the radar screen of my little world and someone would say, "Hey, remember when Bell was here?" and then someone else would give me a friendly shove and say, "Mallory remembers." I'd shrug it off. But every time his name came up I'd feel a little twinge, something I couldn't quite make go away. Those four days we'd had together loomed large in my head, larger than all the days I'd spent with Tommy and all the time I'd spent in Lake Placid combined.

By September, I'd stopped jumping every time the phone rang. I hadn't forgotten Bell, but I was trying to, hard enough that I might have succeeded given another year or two. I might have succeeded if he hadn't shown up on my doorstep in mid-September.

It was a Friday afternoon. I had gone out hiking with Creech and some other friends. I was still waitressing at the Benchmark and after our

41

hike, I had about twenty minutes to shower and get myself over to the restaurant for my shift. It was the beginning of leaf-peeping season, and the Benchmark was so jammed on weekends Leo had asked me to come in early. I'd jumped out of the shower and was standing in front of a foggy bathroom mirror trying to blow dry my hair. When I turned off the blow dryer, I heard a knock. I ran for my robe, stubbed my toe on the bed frame, cursed, and hobbled to answer the door.

I swung it open. Bell was already halfway back down the stairs.

It had been six months since I'd seen him. My heart fluttered around in my chest. I was kidding myself, if I thought six months was long enough to forget him.

"Wait." I couldn't keep the desperation from my voice.

Bell turned and hustled back up the stairs.

We crashed into each other. I buried my face deep into his sweatshirt. He smelled of damp fall air, the slight coolness of being outside. I felt such a mix of things, urgency, longing and anger at his just showing up. Overriding everything was the need to hang on. He didn't let go for a long time and when he finally did, he just backed up a step and looked at me. He kept looking at me, not saying anything. And my anger at being discarded came back.

"I have to go to work." I thought I had found my cool. I wouldn't let him play around with my heart. Not again.

When I popped back out of the bathroom dressed, he was sitting on my bed. I thought about telling him that I wanted him gone when I got back, but the way he sat there, legs splayed apart, looking like he belonged on that bed and knowing I wanted him there, made me change my mind. "I'll be home at ten," I told him.

"Okay," he said. And walking out the door, I realized that was the only word he'd said to me since he walked in.

To say that I was distracted at work would have been an understatement. I nearly dropped a bowl of Leo's French onion soup into the lap of a nicely dressed, older man. As it was, the soup sloshed over the edge of the tureen and landed on my hand. I apologized to the startled man and got him a fresh bowl, all the while shaking the angry red spot on my finger.

"What's with you tonight?" Corky asked.

"Bell's back."

She had a pierced eyebrow, and she sent the little ring dancing towards her hairline. "You're shitting me."

There was a kind of giddiness in her voice, a giddiness I wished I could feel but didn't. I was still reeling from his return, my head a jumble of thoughts, a mix of emotions, which all seemed to tumble back to fear—I'd go home after work and find him gone.

I wished the dinner shift would hurry up and be done, which, of course, just made it go by all the more slowly. When Corky offered to close so that I could go home, I took her up on the offer without an argument.

Bell was there when I got back to the apartment. He was asleep on top of the unmade bed in the clothes he'd come in wearing. His backpack sat right where he'd dropped it near the

43

door. He didn't wake up when I walked in and turned on the light. I turned the light back off and tiptoed around in the dark. There wasn't far to go in my little place, and so I went into the bathroom, shut the door, and sat on the toilet trying to figure out what to do next. I thought about waking him or running over to Corky's to crash for the night. In the end, I changed into the ratty T-shirt I usually slept in and climbed in next to him. I lay there in the dark for the longest time, feeling the warmth of him, listening to him breathe.

I woke to the sound of the shower. The apartment was in an old house and the pipes thrummed and shook any time you turned on a faucet. The shower was especially loud and there was a steady jack hammering to accompany the fall of water.

Bell's clothes, the ones he'd slept in, were dumped at the end of the bed. It didn't take long for Bell to appear at the door naked, using the only towel I had in the bathroom to dry his hair. He finished and the hair dropped into wet blond tangles at his shoulders. I shut my eyes and pretended I was still asleep. I could hear him moving around the room, rummaging through what I assumed was his backpack. There was a faint hint of strawberry in the air—the scent of my shampoo.

"Mallory?"

I rolled over and opened my eyes. He was standing next to the bed in jeans and a crumpled blue T-shirt with a Rossignol logo on it. When he saw I was awake, he sat down. "We should talk."

This sounded to me like the opening line of a breakup. It was, I think, what I said to Tommy when I made my decision to come north. I remember Tommy looked away, because he'd already figured out what was coming next. But Bell and I weren't a couple. We weren't anything but two people who had spent a few days together, even if they were the most memorable days of my life.

"Talk about what?" I asked.

He was sitting close enough to graze my arm. I'd be lying if I said I didn't want him just then.

He lay down next to me on the bed, staring at the ceiling. "I'm AWOL."

I followed suit, my eyes catching a brown water stain above us. The stain looked like a four-leaf clover. I wondered if this was a lucky omen, and then just exactly what lucky might mean.

"I'm supposed to be in Valle Nevado right now."

"What are you talking about?"

"There's not much to explain. I'm supposed to be there, but I'm here."

I propped myself up on my elbows. "Why are you here?"

He looked at me as though it should be self-evident. "I'm not in Chile because I want to be here. I needed to see you."

He got up and walked to the window, which looked downhill to the backside of Main Street. "You ever been to Alaska?"

"No." The sudden change of tack caught me off guard.

"You should go. Those peaks, they fly into the sky. You can feel them." He turned to face me. "That's where I was. Denali. Skiing on Denali, over Wickersham's Wall. There's nothing there but you and the mountain and the sky. The air's so thin you have to gasp at it. The mountain could take you in. Could swallow you, if you let it."

Bell walked back to the bed. He had a look in

his eyes that was far away, as though he wasn't standing there at all. "Powder so thick you couldn't see, edges digging into near nothing, just dancing in the white room, you know?" He sat back down, took my hand, and cradled it into his chest. "Then, after, I'm supposed to go do this commercial shoot in Chile for Pepsi. They wanted me to be there yesterday. All they talk about is timelines and dollars and shit. I got as far as LAX. I'm sitting there on one of those plastic jobs, my bag between my knees, waiting for a plane to Santiago. And it all seemed wrong. Next thing I know, I'm watching that plane take off without me. I knew where I had to go and it wasn't there."

Bell took my shoulders. "Up there, on Denali, I decided I wanted my life to be real. And I wanted to spend it with you."

There was this look in his eyes, the same one he'd come in with last night. A look that comes from having done too much.

"My life's not that fabulous," I said, sweeping over my sad little apartment with my own eyes.

"No, it is. You're doing what you want. You packed up everything so that you could be here, doing what you love in a place you love. I'm hoping there's a place for me, too. In your life."

I didn't know how to answer him.

"Sorry," he said. "It's a lot to lay on you, I know."

"Then why did you lay it on me?" I asked.

"Because I haven't stopped thinking about you for six months."

It wasn't so much what he said, but the way that he said it, the tiny near-inaudible break in his voice, the way his eyes came home, descending from the pitch of that far-off lofty place to nest in mine. I knew I could never refuse those eyes.

Chapter Five

Emily wakes me up in the morning. Because she'd fallen asleep so early the night before, she's raring to go by six. She comes up with Chance and both of them jump on the bed. I groan a little, then laugh and hug them both.

It's still pretty cold, and by lunchtime I'm more than happy to go get Emily and get into the cafeteria. Albie's wife, Eliza, makes soup at least once a week, enough to feed an entire squadron. Albie brings it in to share. He pours out some for Emily and for me, telling Emily all the while that it's good stuff and she ought to eat up. It is good stuff, turkey with rice, little bits of vegetables floating through the broth. Emily steals some crackers from the condiment bar and stirs them into the mix. Albie watches her and me. He'll never ask how I'm getting on, though I can see that maybe he wants to. We talk instead about the hill and soup and kids.

After lunch, I take Emily out for a run. She glides over the same blue square trail we skied with Corky yesterday, and I know she's trying to show me that she's good enough for the summit. I renew my promise to take her after the next snowfall.

I'm glad I didn't take her today. The wind whips up on summit quad as I ride up after dropping Emily off. Up here, even snowmaking doesn't keep the trails from icing. I pass the start house, where Creech is talking to one of his racers. I can imagine what he's saying. He's telling her that she has to be better than good. Races are measured in hundredths of seconds, and it doesn't take much, a wrong-set edge, a wide line, to pull your time off the boards. Creech can be a real bear as a coach, but I know he encourages the girls too. Nobody wants them to succeed more than he does.

I catch his eye and wave as I ski past, running the first two gates, whacking my arm and thigh into the slalom pole before skiing down off the side. The snow at the edge of the trail is loose and easy and riding down it is the best thing I could be doing. I think of Bell again. Precision is important in the skiing he does, too. Only with what he does, a miss set edge or a mistake about what line to take will do more than get a skier disqualified. It could get him dead.

I tell myself to stop it. Bell's been skiing for a long time. He's good at it, arguably the best in the world.

Albie's waiting at the bottom. Next to him is a woman in snow boots and a winter coat that looks like it would be better suited to Manhattan than a ski slope. Her face is pale and she's looking up the hill, past me, then turning to talk in rapid bursts at Albie.

Albie signals me over, and the woman looks at me like I'm some sort of avenging angel. I've got her pegged. She's a lodge mom. A woman who brings her kids up to the hill to ski and waits for them in the lodge with a book and a thermos of coffee. I try to imagine Emily strapping on her boards and going off without me while I wait, and I can't. A lodge mom is something I'll never be.

The woman, whose name is Bethany, is worried about her son and his friend. "They were supposed to come in for lunch at one, and it's after

49

two," she says, trying to keep the panic out of her voice.

I imagine Emily missing for an hour and I can't help but empathize. Losing your kid for an hour would be enough to make any mom buggy.

"Two boys. Twelve-year olds, one on a board and one with skis. Have you seen them?" she asks me.

"Sorry, no" I wasn't looking, and two twelve-year olds on a crowded hill would be easy to miss even if I was.

Albie radios out and puts everyone on alert. "They may have lost track of the time," he tells Bethany. "Kids will do that."

This does not comfort her. "They've never done this before."

"Were they skiing with anyone else?" I ask.

"There are a group of kids at their school who come up here a lot. I don't know whether any of them are here today." Then, sure enough, she spots a girl she recognizes in the lift line. She gets excited, and points the girl out. "That little girl," she says, "I think her name is Kim. She goes to Graham's school. They ski together sometimes."

"Kim," Bethany yells towards the line. Four girls turn and none of them is the right girl. Albie skis up to the Kim who hasn't turned and taps her on the shoulder.

"Kim?" he asks. The girl leans back on her skis, she looks as though she would like to ski away. "I'm Amber," she says. "Kim's my sister." She can barely be heard; she's speaking into her pigtails.

"Do you know Graham Bessinger?" asks Albie.

Bethany, Albie, and I circle the girl.

"Yes," she says, casting a wary eye towards the

two girls who are her lift partners. They've all scooted out of line now, and people are moving around them. One girl, a boarder, stumbles over the tail of Amber's ski and almost falls.

"Have you seen Graham or Kerry Tyrell?" asks Bethany.

The girls all look at each other now. "They were up on top," says the girl with the board. The other two shrug.

Albie's looking at them with his sugar-blue eyes. He's tall, something like six five, and with that shock of white hair and that deep voice, a twelve-year-old is liable to mistake him for God.

"When did you see them?" he asks.

The girls look everywhere but at Albie. The boarder is staring at me, her eyes blinking away like a caution light. She says something too quiet for anyone but her friends to hear. "Jeez, Jen," says Amber.

"What is it, Jen?" Bethany pounces on the opportunity.

Jen draws a sharp breath, her face is red. "They said they were going into the glades," she says, her eyes on her friends. "Kerry dared and Graham and him, they said they were going to go. They dared us too, but we didn't because Marissa's not so good yet."

The one called Marissa gives Jen a hard stare.

"I'll go," I tell Albie, though I'm not thrilled at the prospect of skiing the glades we closed yesterday.

"Take Coyote with you," says Albie.

Bethany's arms fold and unfold as though she can't decide what to do with them. "The glades?" she asks.

I'm on the lift and radioing Coyote before I can

hear Albie explain.

I wait for Coyote on top. He grumbles at the thought of a glade run, voicing exactly what I've been thinking. Normally, I love the glades. But today they are barely skiable, an accident waiting to happen.

"Stupid kids," he mutters as we duck the rope.

We sweep slowly down either side of the narrow trail, where the best snow is piled up against the tree trunks. Twice, I bump rock. I wonder aloud why anyone would think this was fun. The rocks will leave gashes in my skis, huge chunks that will have to be filled in.

Not too far down the trail, in a gully some ten feet deep, I spot them—two kids huddled near a tree. I yell over to Coyote and then sideslip down the gully's steep bank. Ironically, the snow cover down here is better than it is in the glade. There's a snowboard propped up against the tree. The kid who I assume owns the board stands up when he sees us, his boots sinking into the soft snow at the bottom of the gully. The other kid is sitting propped against the tree, one ski on, the other about twenty yards downhill. He's got his boot off, and he's holding his leg. By the looks of it, he's been crying. They both look pretty shell shocked and they seem both happy and scared to see me coming for them.

I take off my skis, plant them, and walk the last few yards toward them, sinking boots deep into the snow.

"Graham hurt his leg," the snowboarder tells me.

"You Kerry?" I ask.

The kid nods, surprised. "How'd you know my name?"

"They're looking for you down at the bottom."

I radio Albie to tell him we've found the boys and it looks like we're going to need the sled. While Coyote works his way down the embankment, I take off the kid's other ski. "This the leg?" I ask, taking up the one the kid is holding.

The kid nods.

I slide my hands down his lower leg, exerting pressure every couple of inches. "Where does it hurt?"

"Down here, by my ankle."

I run my hands over his ski sock and press just above the top of it.

"Ow," he says.

Coyote got his skis off now and he's kneeling down next to me. "We have a possible Maisonneuve fracture. We're going to need an air splint," I tell him.

"What's wrong with it?" asks Graham, fighting back fresh tears.

"It looks like you broke your leg," I say. When I move the foot gently, tears stream down Graham's face. His friend watches, pale and serious.

Albie's voice crackles over the radio. "I'm sending Turk Millet with the sled."

I do an inward groan that Coyote catches. He's not too fond of Turk Millet either.

Turk, for all his faults, is a great skier. But he's inexperienced, and I worry about him carrying the toboggan down over these rocks. I'm also less than thrilled because I'm one of only two women working fulltime patrol on the hill, and Turk sees fit to harass me at every turn.

I'm used to being a girl in a boy's world. I learned early that the best way to shut them up was to out ski them. I learned that back when I was a kid. At Ridge Run, there was a ten-foot rock that sat right under the chairlift near the top of the trail. You were supposed to ski around it, of course, but the bunch I was skiing with decided it would be more fun to jump it. There were six of us, and we were all about ten years old at the time. I was the only girl. One by one, the boys chickened out. But I got up on the top of the slope, pointed my skis downhill and took off. My heart was pounding. I was in the air for a long time. It felt like flying. After sticking the landing, I had to turn a hard left to avoid a head on with a maple tree. Creech followed me, jumping the rock. The others followed him. Three of them fell on the landing. I never heard another word from any of them about being a girl. I only wish it were that easy with guys like Turk.

His voice crackles over the radio now. "I'm bringing the sled down on the Cat."

The Arctic Cat is a snowmobile that we sometimes use for rescue.

I survey the exposed rocks. "Bad idea, Turk. You'll break the Cat and the sled."

"I can't maneuver the sled down there by myself."

I hold the radio away from my face and count to ten before answering him. "Then find someone to help you. We could use a couple of extra hands on our end too."

"There's nobody else at the station."

Coyote grabs the radio from me. "Do not bring the Cat down here unless you plan on using your next four paychecks to repair the sucker. Find someone to come down with you."

"Will do."

I shake my head at the radio. "Will do?"

"I think Turk might be short for Turkey," says Coyote.

54

I pull up Graham's ski pants and the long johns underneath. The skin under his knee is discolored and the leg has begun to swell. I pull the pant back down over it. I pull the sock back up. "We'll get you out of here in a few minutes," I tell him. "You guys warm enough?" I ask, because both kids have started shaking.

I pull a space blanket from my pack and wrap it around Graham. "Kerry, zip up and put your mittens on. You need to stay warm." The last thing we need is frostbite or hypothermia. I radio down to Albie. "We've got a fracture in the proximal fibula. It might be a Maisonneuve."

A Maisonneuve fracture is a nasty injury. It happens when the foot is held fixed while the leg rotates. I'd bet the kid also has some torn ligaments along with a broken leg. In any case, he'll be riding in the ambulance to the local emergency room.

"The bus is standing by," Albie says.

Coyote turns to Kerry. "Grab your friend's other ski for me, buddy."

I know he does this to get Kerry moving again and the kid looks relieved to have something to do.

I hear swearing and turn to see Turk standing at the top of the incline. Sully's behind him, the sled between them. Maybe he can follow directions after all. "We are never going to get this fucker down there," says Turk. "You'll have to come to us."

"Fine. But we have to splint the leg first." Turk grabs the splint and pitches it. It lands five feet up, catching on a bush. Coyote retrieves it, muttering something under his breath.

We splint Graham's leg. "Okay, Graham, Coyote and I are going to carry you to the sled. On my count—one, two, three." Coyote and I do a fireman's hold—we form a chair around the kid and hoist him up. He's pretty heavy, and I think it would probably have been better to let Sully or Turk help with the carry, but I'm not about to lay my reputation on the line. We struggle up the slope and get Graham secured onto the sled. Coyote takes the kid's skis over his shoulder. "Hang on," Sully tells the kid. "You get the fun part."

Kerry's climbed up behind us, leaving his board down in the gully and he looks like he's going to cry. "How do I get out of here?" he asks, casting nervous glances at his friend.

"Only way out is down," I tell him. He does not look thrilled with my answer.

Kerry looks with longing at the sled, which must seem the better deal to him now.

"I'll help you get to the bottom." I tell him. It's not far to the chute, which will link us onto the open trail.

The others take off slowly, Turk in the lead guiding the sled, picking his way through the trees. I begrudgingly allow he's being pretty careful.

"Go get your board," I tell Kerry. He does, though he looks leery of strapping it back on. "You can probably walk this part." I push back into my bindings. "I'll stay with you. We'll go to the chute."

He looks like he doesn't know what I'm talking about. I point down to where the sled has disappeared through a line of trees. "We have to stay to the right."

I'd bet a year's salary he's never skied the glades before, and he chose a hell of a time to start. He carries his board and we start picking through the trees. My ski grazes another rock.

The trail next to the chute is marked Double Black Diamond, Experts Only. It's steep and pretty rutted, with a deep tangle of moguls up the spine.

We come out about halfway down. Below us is the runoff, a wide trail that is much flatter and easier to negotiate. "Okay, let's go," I say, relieved to be out of the trees.

Kerry looks like he's going to cry again. "I've never been on this one," he blurts.

"Never?"

He shakes his head, and suddenly he seems about Emily's age. I want to yell at him, ask him what he thinks he's doing in the glades if he can't handle the regular terrain, but I hold my tongue. By rights, I could confiscate his lift ticket. That's the usual fine for skiing a closed trail, and the glades were clearly marked closed. As Albie likes to say, them's the rules. But the kid is so clearly shaken by this experience I don't have the heart. Besides, his friend will be taking a trip to the hospital, and this kid's ski day is pretty much over anyway.

I help him pick his way down the side of the trail, where the moguls aren't as big and there's better snow. It's hard, because I'm not a boarder, but I get him to sideslip on the board. He goes slowly, scraping snow off the surface of ice as he descends. It takes what seems like an eternity to get to the runoff. From there, it's clear sailing, though the kid's still having a little trouble. He's been boarding way out of his league, and the shaky knees don't help.

The ambulance is waiting by the time we get back to first aid. Bethany's standing next to the ambulance entrance of the station, a purse and two equipment bags tangled in her arms as Albie and Coyote get Graham ready for transport.

"End of the line," I tell Kerry.

He smiles, relieved, the minute before Graham's mother gives him a foul look. He and

Graham will get an earful before this is all over, I think. And next season, they'll be back ducking the ropes again.

Turk smirks at me as they put Graham into the back of the ambulance. I count to ten again. So far, I've contained myself, but if he pushes any harder, we're going to have a showdown before the season's out.

Chapter Six

I give Emily her bath, needed because she's missed a day, and get her ready for bed. In footy pajamas, her hair wet and smelling of baby shampoo, she's the little girl that I sometimes forget she is. We go through a ritual closet stomp before bed. She's convinced a monster lives in her closet and so we open the door every night and yell at him. "You get out of here, monster!!" we say and then we stomp our feet three times and growl, which always makes Emily giggle.

Settled into bed, she asks for a story and I start for a book. "No, not that one, Mommy," she says. "I want the story of Daddy and the mountain."

This stops me for a minute. I have to bite my lip to keep from crying. "I don't know that one, Em."

"Yes you do. Daddy went to the big mountain," she begins and she lies back expectantly.

I swallow hard. "Oh, that one," I say and I pick up as best I can. "Daddy went to the big mountain. It's in a place that's far away."

"Alaska," says Emily.

"That's right. Alaska. Where it's always cold and snowy."

"And there's people live in snow houses."

"That's right. They're called igloos."

"Will Daddy live in an igloo?"

"Some of the time. And sometimes in a tent."

"And what's the big mountain called?" she asks, though I know she already knows the answer.

"It's called Denali." The name is loose and

pliable on my tongue. It rolls like pebbles in my mouth.

"And there's a big wall. Tall as the tallest tallest. And Daddy's going down down down in the snow."

She's got the facts a little confused here, but I'm not up to correcting her. "That's right, honey," I say. "Daddy's going to be the first one to ski down it."

"Mommy." Emily's voice is heavy with sleep. "When I get big I'm going to ski down the big wall too."

The house grows quiet after she falls asleep. I go to the kitchen and make a cup of tea, then carry it upstairs. Bell has a website for the expedition, and I check it for the first time since he's left. There are some file photos, nothing's changed. I lie on the bed and pick up a copy of *Couloir Magazine* from the floor on Bell's side. I page through. Too many steep vertical drops for my liking. I lay it back down and snuggle into my pillow.

I think about how hard it was when Bell came back from his last run in with the West Rib. It took months for him to recover. In the spring, when he was finally back to normal, we backpacked the Northville Placid trail in celebration. It was still a little cold, and there were patches of snow and ice along the way. We slept in a tent Bell had used in Alaska and joked about how climbing into the sleeping bags we'd zipped together was the only way to keep warm. It took us three weeks to hike the trail, just the two of us in the woods.

We ran out of trail mix, which wasn't a big deal.

And we ran out of condoms, which, it turned out, was.

60

I go back and look in on Emily. Her blonde hair fans the pillow. She smiles in her sleep. I have no regrets about having her. Though, sometimes, I wonder that I'm a mother. That I'm capable of taking care of her at all.

I wasn't going to tell Bell I was pregnant. Not at first. When my period was late, I got one of those kits at the drugstore. I peed on the stick and it changed color. Hard evidence. I threw the thing in the trash, buried it and the box under a wad of tissues. I went around in a fog for a few days. I didn't tell anyone. Finally, I called Planned Parenthood and made an appointment. It was my problem and I would solve it.

When the day for my appointment came, I sat in the Jeep and started crying. Weeping was more like it.

The next I knew, Bell climbed into the seat beside me. He put his hand to the back of my neck, rubbed softly "What's wrong, baby?"

"I'm pregnant."

"Oh," he said, "Wow."

He got out of the truck and looked off towards Mount Marcy as though he were thinking over the whole sorry situation. Then he sighed and went into the house.

The room that was to become Emily's was our storage room. Between us, we have a sports shop's worth of ski equipment and camping and climbing gear. The room was a tangled mess of tents and ropes and poles.

I found Bell standing in the middle of it.

"I'll build a garage for all this stuff," he said. "We can fix up this room." He came over to me, put his hand to my still concave belly and kissed my forehead. "We can paint it yellow."

Bell calls from Talkeetna. He tells me it's cold and they're snowed in. They won't go out to the base camp on Kahiltna Glacier until the snow lets up. The base camp is eight thousand feet up, the beginning of a long climb to the summit at twenty-one thousand feet. Bell, Roddie, and the other six members of the team will stay at base camp for a week to get acclimated. The crew will stay behind when Bell, Roddie, and two others, Jerome Cantrell and Jack Bernes, try for the top. Roddie will head the climbing team and Bell is the only one who will attempt to ski down. Like all teams, Bell's has a name. They call themselves 'Emily's Boys'.

Talkeetna is a tiny town, population about three hundred, and it's over one hundred miles from the mountain. But it's Denali park base, the place where all climbs begin. In the summer climbing season, it is overrun with those who want to make the trek up Denali's formidable sides. Bell and his team chose to do the ascent and ski in March, a good month before climbing season begins. All the more dangerous that way, and all the more likely to make the record books as a first.

I can tell Bell is itching to get started. His frustration at being stuck in Talkeetna comes through even as he asks how things are at home and waits for my reply. I'm ready to make a stab at this conversation despite myself. There's no turning him around now, though I'm still hoping for an apology I'm pretty sure will never come.

"Kid dixied up in the glades today," I tell him. "It was roped off. It's a mess of rock and mud. We could use some of that snow."

"I'd send it to you, if I could. I ducked the rope

a few times when I was a kid."

"But you didn't land against a tree." I tell him about the gully, the sled, the snowboarder friend.

"Been there." And he tells me how he skied, then fell, into a ravine off one side of the mountain. "My knee in a tree." He laughs. "But I've learned a few things since then."

I want to ask exactly what it is he thinks he's learned. Seems to me he's still ducking the ropes and skiing down ravines. I change the subject instead. "Me and Em are going up to Danny's tomorrow."

There's a little bit of a pause on the phone. The line crackles and I think about how far away he is and I think about how much I want him here right now.

"It's good, you're going up there," Bell says.

On these trips, I bring Danny groceries, firewood, and a paper. If Bell were here, he'd come with me. I like to think it helps Danny out. He's ninety three, and he refuses to even think about leaving his cabin out in the woods. Bell and I have discussed putting an addition on our own cabin, but Danny won't hear of it. He'll go out in those woods, and maybe that's as it should be. A transfer would probably kill him. It would surely kill his spirit and isn't that the same thing?

"You know Danny," I tell Bell. "He'll go to Agway to buy food for the dogs, but he won't stop at the market for bread."

Bell laughs and then there's another pause. I don't want to say goodbye. I don't want to lose his voice, though part of me is still mightily pissed that he's put me here, on this phone with him out there, in the first place.

"It'll be hard to call from base camp. But I can

try, if you want."

I do want that and because I do, his offer is causing a meltdown. I don't answer him.

"Mallory, you still there?"

I swallow the tears. "Yeah, I'm here. It'd be good, if you called. If you want."

"I'll be home soon. You won't have time to miss me." He's giving me the same play that he's been giving me for weeks, since long before he left.

"Maybe you can talk to Em, if you call again."

His voice brightens. "How is my munchkin?"

"She's talking about you."

"Yeah?"

"By tomorrow, she'll be asking to see your old ski movies."

"You'll show them to her?"

"Sure. We'll make popcorn and watch." I pause. Then I decide to say it anyway, the thing that's there in the front of my head. "Bell, don't dixie on us."

There's a sigh on the other end of the line. "Jesus, Mallo. Don't start again."

And there we are, right back to where we were when he left.

Chapter Seven

"You're raising demons," says Danny, handing me a cup of coffee. We're in his cabin; the groceries that I bought for him earlier have been packed away in the knotted pine kitchen. Emily's outside romping around with the dogs. I watch the place where the linoleum peels as it meets the wood floor of what used to be Danny's living room, which is his bedroom now.

"The blizzard in Talkeetna isn't just in my imagination." I try to keep the hitch out of my voice. It's there despite my efforts.

"You worry over PD too much." His ancient eyes are bright blue, just like his grandson's.

"I'm not worried," I lie. I can see in his face he's not buying.

"PD can take care of himself," he says as he shuffles over to the refrigerator for milk. He sloshes some into his cup and then hands the carton to me. It's wet and leaves a mark on the Formica table, which, like the floor, is cracked near the edges and could use a good scrubbing. I make a mental note to get the Ajax out after lunch. If I don't make a fuss about it, he might let me scrub.

There's a pot of navy bean soup warming on the stove. I bought it in the deli department of the grocery because I know it's Danny's favorite, though I don't much care for it. I hope that Emily will eat it.

I look out the window to check on her, and there she is, scooting around the backyard with

Chance and Danny's chocolate lab, Ella.

"Better drink up while she's still hot," says Danny pointing to my coffee. He follows my gaze and shakes his head. "She's growing up too fast, the little munchkin."

I wonder if he's thinking about his own Emily, Bell's mother, who did grow up too fast. She was only seventeen when she had Bell. She didn't live long either. Died in a car crash when Bell was six. I make a silent vow to shelter my little girl.

Danny puts his hand on mine as though he's reading my thoughts. The hand is dry and leathery. I wonder if Bell will look like Danny old. I wonder if Bell will make it to old.

"He'll come around, you'll see," says Danny.

"What?"

"PD. He'll come back. He belongs here with you and Emily. He'll have his adventure and he'll be back."

"I don't know, Danny. It's always some big adventure with him. Who knows what's next? Someday he might just not bother to come home."

Danny withdraws his hand and gives me a stern look. "You underestimate him." He's always supported Bell, even Bell at his craziest.

I go to the stove and give the soup a stir. "Lunch's almost ready."

"Let me tell you a story," says Danny, unwilling to drop it. I put the spoon down on the range top and look at him. I feel like shrugging him off, but I don't.

"When PD was about ten, he wanted to paint his room. Blue, because that's his favorite color. Now I told him we would paint. But not right then because money was tight.

"That kid went up to the hill and entered a

mogul contest. Most of the skiers in it were grown and twice his size. He come down that trail like he was on fire, and damned if he didn't win. Twenty-dollar gift certificate to the ski shop, which he traded for cash. He went to the hardware and bought paint. Damn room's still blue."

Danny chuckles and I'm left wondering what this tale has to do with anything at all. Sometimes I swear the old man is getting squirrelly. I ladle soup into three bowls and put crackers on the table.

"Point is, Mallory," he says seeing that he's lost me. "That boy gets something in his head and he's going to do it." This I didn't need to be told. "If I'm not wrong, that's one of the best things about him."

I want to tell him the apple doesn't fall far, he and Bell are both as stubborn as the day is long, but I like Danny and I don't want to pick a fight with him, so I don't say it. I call Emily and she comes bounding in all rosy-cheeked with Chance and Ella at her heels. Danny's other dog, a retriever named Birdie, looks up and wags her tail from her spot near the stove. In dog years, Birdie's near as old as Danny.

We change subjects and talk about the weather. Danny's shed roof has folded under the snow and he's ready to rebuild. I know better than to offer to help him, but I do offer to go to the lumberyard with him. "Maybe come April," says Danny. "Once the snow's gone. PD will be back by then." And we're talking about Bell again. It's like he never left the conversation.

On the way home, Emily asks why Grandpa Danny lives up in the woods all alone. "He likes living out in the woods," I tell her, "and he's got his dogs to keep him company."

Emily thinks this over for a while. She seems

satisfied with the answer. She scratches Chance behind the ears. "You're good company, too, Chancie."

"Mom?" she says when we are nearly home. "If Danny is Daddy's grandpa, where's his daddy?"

There's one I don't have an easy answer for.

Bell's lack of father isn't a burden he carries lightly. His mom got pregnant as a teenager, and she refused to tell anyone who the father was. A psychologist would have a field day, because Bell ought to have all kinds of issues around this. Truth is Bell isn't much of an issues guy. He's not angst-ridden, he's not angry and, although he does play it fast and loose sometimes, he is not entirely crazy.

When we first talked about our families, a day or two after we met during those first four days we had together, I told him about my parents. About how they didn't seem to really like each other and how I could never figure out why they had gotten together in the first place. They divorced when I was sixteen, and my first thought about it wasn't 'oh, my God,' it was more like 'thank God.' They are really much better apart than they ever were together. Bell kind of nodded along when I spouted all this.

"My mom died," he told me. "And I don't have a father." He was very matter-of-fact about it, said it like it didn't scorch him in the least.

But even then, when I'd only known him for a few days, I could tell it did bother him. Maybe a lot. I let the subject drop.

It never came up between us again until Emily came along. Bell stayed home the January she was born. He wanted to be there and he made it a point that he was. We hadn't picked out any names, and a couple of weeks before she splashed down, I was thumbing through a baby names book Corky had given us trying to come up with something. Bell took the book from me.

"I know what I'd like to call her if it's a girl." He put his hand to my belly and traced the wide arch it made under my shirt. "Emily. It was my mom's name."

I wouldn't have said no even if his mom's name had been Ferdinand. And our daughter's been Emily ever since. It suits her since she is so much like Bell.

That summer, when Emily was about six months old, Bell had her out in the yard. He was twirling her around and she was giggling. Chance, who was only a puppy then, danced around them both.

"Say Daddy," said Bell, "Daa-dey" When he saw that I was watching, he stopped and looked sheepish. I smiled at them both.

"Girl's got a terrific daddy."

"Least she's got one." Bell's look had gone serious.

"You ever think about finding him?"

Bell balanced the baby on his hip. "He clearly doesn't want to be found."

"Maybe he does. Maybe he never knew."

Bell shook his head. "It's no good, Mallo, opening up old hurts." He tousled the baby's fine hair. "But I don't intend to make the same mistake with her."

Chapter Eight

It's been four days since Bell called from Talkeetna. I wait, agonizing it was my remark, the one that sent us back to the same old argument that keeps him from calling. I'm pretty sure he doesn't want to talk to me because of it, because he thinks talking about his big fall will jinx him. It busts me that he hasn't called for Emily. Not that she's waiting. She figures he's gone and he'll be back. Like he always is.

I check the website every day. The snowstorm ended Tuesday. A few days ago they flew out to the glacier and set up base. So that's it. They've arrived.

It's the last day of February, and there's a heavy fog here this morning that sticks to the mountaintops. The chairlifts disappear into it. Tomorrow, we'll turn the calendar page, but it won't be spring here, not yet. Just a mix of cold and the warm trying to get born.

Spring comes slowly here, the transition unruly and guarded; more snow, some wind, then the mud will come and muck up our front steps and suck at our boots. Another month will pass and there'll be a quick step to heat and black flies, while summer waits in the wings.

I love this time of year on the hill. The days are longer and warmer. The crowds thin to a die-hard few. The craziness in all of us comes out; we ski in shorts and tank tops. The moguls are thick, the slush like syrup, deep and heavy. There's good snow if you know where to look. And tricky snow. Changeable, it varies slope to slope, turn to turn. You have to be ready for it, which is both the challenge and the joy of it.

We get a call late in the day. Someone's taken a pretty good tumble up by the Freeway chair. We've spent most of the day sunning ourselves on the lifts, breezing down the trails, and generally taking it easy. End of the day is always busier. People get tired and accidents happen. I go to the crash site. A man, probably in his thirties, is lying in the snow. A woman is standing next to him. There's a red stain on the snow and on his jacket. The blood's running from his nose. In his dixie down, the guy's bopped himself in the nose with his ski pole. His wife is really worried about this, but I tell her it's not a big problem. I did the same thing once when I was a kid. Those blows always seem to cause gushers. They always look much worse than they are. I give the guy an ice pack and go on to check for further injuries. And I find something that really is a worry. His leg is swollen and sensitive and there's a protrusion. The bone poking out of his thigh. He says it doesn't hurt unless I touch it, which isn't as uncommon as it might sound. The pain will set in soon enough.

The snow is wet and heavy, which causes another problem, since his wind pants are a narrow defense against the cold. I wrap a space blanket around him and call for a sled. The trail we're on is a wide blue square, intermediate level trail, easy to get in and out. Nothing like the tree rescue we did last Sunday. But the leg's in bad shape and it's going to take a lot of finesse not to jostle it around.

I cut through the wind pants. The woman, whose name is Julia, catches a glimpse at the mess that is her husband Jeff's leg. She goes a little white, and I'm afraid I'm going to have two cases of hypothermia on my hands. I splint the leg, taking care not to move the bone, and ask them both if they are warm enough. Julia says she's fine, but her teeth are chattering so I give her my jacket and hunker down next to Jeff. And we wait. Ten minutes. Then fifteen. The sun is sinking and it's getting colder by the minute. Jeff is wet from the slushy snow and begins to shiver involuntarily. I wrap the space blanket tighter and we wait some more. My watch says four o'clock. The lifts will be closing soon. Spending a night on the slope could be deadly, even late in the season. I call for the sled again, impatient because it should have been here by now.

"Turk was up top when you radioed first time," says Albie from base. "Isn't he there yet?"

"No, he isn't. And it's getting a little chilly out here." What I want to say is—make him drag his sorry ass down here pronto.

Minutes pass, and I see Turk coming down the trail. Sledless.

"No sled up top," he says.

I ignore him and call Albie. "We need a sled, Albie," I say, not looking at Turk.

"Sully's following up," Albie crackles back. "He's on his way."

Turk is looking at the insignia on the front of his ski.

"Go on down and make sure transport's ready," I tell him. Transport is ready, I'm sure of it. Whoever is down at the station will have seen to it. It's my way of getting rid of Turk, and he knows it.

"Fine," he says, and he roars off down the slope.

I am way past mad, but I tell Julia and Jeff not to worry. I can see Sully guiding the sled towards us with Coyote right behind him. We get Jeff situated and make our way slowly to the bottom.

It's well past five by the time we get it all settled. I've got to pick Emily up at the nursery. I should have been there fifteen minutes ago, but I'm too peeved to go down there right away. I've put up with Turk's shit all winter. And I've had just about enough of it.

I light into him at the aid station, grabbing his shoulder before he can leave, which is no easy task because he's a lot taller than me. "What the hell is wrong with you?"

The place gets very quiet. Kristen Anglers is sitting at the table with Albie and Coyote and Joe McGintock. They're all looking at me.

Turk shoves my arm away. "What's wrong with you?" he says, his lips pulled tight over his teeth.

"Twenty minutes. I waited twenty minutes up there with that guy. He was shaking, for Christ sakes. We are damned lucky he didn't go into shock. Is that why you signed on? So you could single-handedly kill people?" My voice has gone up four decibels. Anybody within a half mile of the station probably heard me.

"The guy is fine. His vitals are good. He's fine."

"No thanks to you. If it were up to me, you would be out of here. You would have been out of here a long time ago with all the shit you pull."

"He's fine. So get off my fucking case."

Then he's out the door. I want to run after him and deck him.

Everyone's staring at me, but I don't care.

"I've got to go get Emily," I say and leave before anyone can make a comment.

Charlotte is coloring with Emily at the table in the nursery room. Em's the only kid left in the place.

"Time to go," I say, still feeling steamed. "Sorry I'm late, Charlotte. Thanks for waiting."

I'm a little abrupt, though I don't mean to be. Charlotte doesn't deserve my anger. I give her a meager smile.

Albie catches me outside the nursery. "Let's go get a coffee," he says.

"I should get the munchkin home."

"A few minutes, Mallory." He's giving me a look that says not sitting down with him is not an option.

The cafeteria is closed. They've put the chairs and benches on top of the tables and a couple of kids are mopping up. Albie goes to Zach, who runs the cafeteria kitchen, and comes back with two coffees and a cocoa for Em. We pull down a couple of chairs and sit. I'm beginning to feel like a kid who's been called into the principal's office.

Albie sips his coffee. The tension is about to kill me, though I know for a fact that I didn't sputter anything the others weren't already thinking.

"Hey, Em." Albie points to the counter. "I think Zach's got a couple of those giant cookies stashed back there. Why don't you go see if you can get us one?" And Em rushes off in search of M&M cookies. "You were a little harsh back there, Mallory," he says, once she's gone.

I'm not feeling contrite. "He's been bruising me all winter, Albie."

Albie nods. "He's having a rough time. He's not

sure he can cut it. And you scare the hell out of him."

This is news. I don't think of myself as scary. "He needs to learn to act like a professional. I'm sick to death of guys who are so cocksure they know what they're doing when they're don't."

I stop myself. I'm not talking about Turk anymore.

Albie takes my arm. "Just ease up a little, Mallo."

I can't even answer him.

"I know things have been a little edgy for you," Albie says. "You've been here a long time. You're the best I've got, Mallo. There's a rescue, I want you out there. No one on the hill is going to disagree with that. Thing is, I can't afford World War III around here. You're wound up pretty tight these days. And it's not like you."

There's a mild throb in my head. I have been upset, but I thought I was being cool, professional. I didn't realize how easy I was to read. First Danny, now Albie. I'm an open book. I put my head in my hands.

"I know Turk's been a pain in your side," Albie says. "But he's got a lot to offer and I think, given time, he's going to be great at his job."

I don't look at him.

"Like you," he adds, and I think he is just doing this to ease things.

Emily comes bounding back over to the table, a huge cookie in either hand. "Zach gave me two, cause I got two hands."

"Here, give me the cookies. You can't eat them right now."

"Why?" Emily's lips draw up into a pout.

"It's almost dinner time."

"And so?"

I'm about ready to yell at her and take the cookies away. But I catch Albie looking at me, and I see what he sees and it's not a very pretty sight.

I pull my little girl onto my lap. "You should ask Albie if he wants some."

"Want some?" she asks, holding out one cookie to Albie.

"No thanks, sugar," says Albie.

"You want some, Mommy?" she asks, generous now.

"No thanks," I say. "What do you say we wrap one up for before bed." I give her a little squeeze. "And you can have the other after pizza?"

"Can I have two bites now?"

"One bite."

She considers this and then takes a huge chunky bite of one of the cookies. "Okay," she says with her mouth full.

Albie's smiling at us. "See you girls tomorrow?"

"You betcha," I say, not feeling quite as excited about the prospect as I'd like to be.

Albie puts a hand to my shoulder. "Don't eat too much pepperoni," he says to Emily.

I decide to take Em to the House of Pizza. I prefer Carducci's, but a lot of people hang there after work and I'm not in the mood for their company. On a whim, I take a ride up Creech's road. His truck's in the drive and the porch light is on.

"Let's see if Creech wants pizza," I say to Em.

Creech answers the door dressed in a fresh pressed shirt and jeans. "Oh, it's you," he says when he sees the two of us.

"I love you too, Creature," I tell him eyeing the outfit. "Hot date?"

He colors a little. "Matter of fact."

"I thought Bunny What's-Her-Name went home to Minerva Falls." I can't help smiling. Leave it to Creech to date someone named Bunny.

"Geneva Falls. And she has gone home. I'm having dinner with Kristen."

"Anglers?"

He colors a little bit more.

"Really?"

"Yes, really, Prescott."

I shake my head.

"What?"

"Nothing. Have a terrific time." I usher Emily back into the car.

Kristen Anglers has been on the patrol for about three years. She's levelheaded, even tempered, and good at her job. She and I are the only two full-time patrolwomen on the hill, and I like that she can hold her own. I never would have imagined Creech was interested in her though. We all go out sometimes, after work, but I've never seen him even flirt with any of the women on staff. I always figured he liked tourist types; girls like Bunny who come up for a week or two and then go home. He's as much as stated this preference with his hundred-mile rule. Creech prides himself on living an uncomplicated life, and I would have bet money that he preferred uncomplicated relationships. That's why I'm a little surprised that he's asked Kristen to dinner.

House of Pizza is no great shakes for ambience and Emily's a little antsy, so I get the pizza and a couple of salads to go. After dinner and the cookie, Em wants to go to the 'Daddy Site,' which is her new name for Bell's expedition website. I tell her she can after her bath and she washes up quickly, which is a good thing, though she's impatient with me when I wash her hair.

The site hasn't been updated since we checked it last night, except for the weather report. It's ten below on Kahiltna Glacier. And ten below is balmy for the glacier. It can get a lot colder and snowier. Bell's good at what he does, I remind myself. He's good at winning against the elements.

Sometimes, though, the elements win.

Chapter Nine

I'm pretty worn out, so after I get Em to sleep I put myself to bed. But I can't seem to settle my brain and I wind up laying there with the lights on and staring at the walls. They are Roaring Mountain Blue, a color we picked as much for the name as for the shade. I give up on the idea of sleep and get up and wander around the house. I stand for a time and look out my window. Beyond the yard there's a hemlock stand, and beyond that the mountains. It's dark now, but I can see them, looming in shadow, the wind tossing the boughs, the peaks dense in the moonlight. I love the view here. I always have, right from the first time I saw it.

The firewood Bell split lies in a discordant heap near the porch. I promise myself I'll stack it on the porch on Monday, my day off. I can already see it corded into a neat pile. Something in me is searching for that kind of order. This small thing I can control even if I can't control Bell's future. But in the next breath it occurs to me we may not need the wood. It'll nearly be spring by the time Bell gets back. Just a few more weeks, I tell myself. Another month.

On a Saturday in mid-October, about a month after Bell went AWOL and came to stay in my apartment, we went to Copperas Pond, scene of our first date. We hiked in a lot farther this time, up and down through hardwood stands, past hemlocks and birches and maples. The leaves were mostly gone from the trees and the sun ricocheted in and out of the branches, swooping over moss-covered rocks and spent leaves. It was cool, winter closes in early around here, and in the clearing by the pond we could see the peaks dotted with snow.

We tramped along, hand in hand, until we came to the edge of a pond. We stood there for a while looking out at the mirror surface of water, the bare tree branches.

"Feels good to be home." Bell put his arm around my waist.

"You're leaving in a few days. The shoot in Chile."

Bell pulled me to face him and pushed a strand of hair back from my face. "I'm not going." He kissed the top of my head. "What I want right now is to be here with you."

"Your dreams have come true," I joked.

"I'm serious. I'm tired of not having an address."

"Kinda comes with the territory, doesn't it?"

"I'm quitting the circuit."

This was news. I stepped back. "For sure?"

Bell laughed. "Yeah, for sure. You remember Rod Kirchman? We've been talking about starting a guide business."

"Sounds like you've got it all worked out."

"I've been thinking about it a lot." He took my face into his hands. "I want to wake up every morning to those pretty green eyes of yours. I belong here. I plan to stay."

"I'd like it, if you stayed."

He kissed me and the kiss felt like a promise.

I switched on the radio on the way home. An old song by Roy Orbison, "Only the Lonely." We sang along and laughed at how badly both of us sang.

Bell stopped mid-verse. "Did you see that?"

I looked around. "See what?"

Bell had already pulled over. He flipped the truck into reverse and backed up over the intersection of an old dirt road until we were parked under a "Land for Sale" sign. "Five acres, ready to build," it said, with an arrow pointing down the road.

"Kismet." Bell smiled. "Want to look?"

The sun was still high in the picture-perfect sky, what better way to spend an afternoon? "Sure."

We bumped down the badly rutted and narrow road, until we came to a large clearing.

"Looks like someone planned to build here," I said as we got out of the truck.

"In the middle of a pine stand. Nice." Bell took my hand and we walked to the middle of the clearing. The view was spectacular. "Is that Mount Marcy?" I pointed to the tallest of the mountains surrounding us. Mt. Marcy was the highest peak in the state.

Bell nodded. "Tawahus. That's what the Indians called it. It means cloud splitter."

The name is apt. The mountain usually wears a crown of cloud, though on this day the sky was an iridescent blue and the peak stuck out glistening clear wearing a napkin of snow.

"This is about the prettiest place I've ever seen," I told Bell.

We explored around. Just beyond the copse of pine was a tiny brook, thick with rocks. In this season, no more than a trickle of water flowed through it and we stepped across it easily. We sat on a rock by that brook and breathed in the pine.

"It is nice, isn't it?" said Bell.

We went home and nothing else was said about the land. It had been fun exploring out there, a nice cap for a near-perfect day, and I figured that's where it would stay. Until I came home from work later that week to find Bell sprawled across the bed with a bunch of drawing paper. He had been sketching something. On closer inspection, I saw it was a house. A cabin with a front porch running along the length of it.

"Like it?" he asked, handing me the sketch. "I'm going to build it. You can buy these log kits at a place down in Keene. Danny built his place and so can we. I'll get some people to help. You, and maybe Creech, and some of the other guys from the hill."

"You want to build a cabin?"

"Yes. We can start before the snow and get the shell up. Do the inside work once it gets cold."

"A cabin?" I asked again.

He grinned. "Yeah. Isn't it great?" He shuffled through some other papers and handed one of them to me. A sales contract.

"What's this?" I asked.

"That land in North Elba. I'm going to buy it." He beamed like a kid who'd just received the world's best Christmas present. "I made an offer and they've accepted. I wanted to surprise you. We can't live here forever."

Forever is a long time and Bell has never been one for timekeeping. And when he said 'forever,' I didn't think he was serious about staying put. But we closed on the land a week later, the deed in both our names at Bell's insistence. And within another week, Bell began to build us a house.

It took six weeks to do the exterior. Bell went to Saranac every morning to pick up Danny. They'd stop at the donut place on the way to the house site and Bell would buy Danny a chocolate cream and a coffee. Danny called it his pay. "Best the kid can do," he'd joke, but you could see how proud he was of Bell and how pleased he'd been asked to help out.

There were half a dozen people out there on any given day. Word got out, and everybody knew somebody who knew something about building. Bell was in the middle of it all, tool belt slung over his hips. Danny taught me how to measure and saw. Bell taught me about tongue and groove, how every log fit neatly into the one next to it. I loved the place even before it became whole, loved working under the shadow of Tawahus, loved the way the wood smelled on those fiercely bright autumn days. It snowed mid-November and we kept going. By Thanksgiving I was back on the hill fulltime, along with most of the help, and Bell and Danny worked away with whatever crew they could muster from first light to last.

In December, Bell went to Chamonix for a week. He had a couple of other shoots that winter. The money was good. Bell had been attracting major money for a couple of years. He lived quietly, with little overhead, and could have retired easily by the time he left to run his guide company, X-tremes. Though I can't imagine Bell retired.

By February, the house was finished. We moved in on a brittle day. It took less than an hour to move our stuff in. Most of what we owned was equipment. We could inventory our furniture using one hand—a mattress, a dresser, a desk, and a chair. Bell fired up the wood stove in the great room and the whole place smelled of wood smoke and fresh pine.

"Close your eyes," Bell said. He took my hand and led me up the stairs. There, along the center wall under the skylight, stood a bed frame, the headboard made of interlaced birch branches.

"It's beautiful." I ran my fingers along the branches and then along the line of his face.

"I'm glad you like it." He took my hand, and we lay down on the floor where the bed would be and made love under the frame.

Over the years, Bell has made a table and chairs, a rocker, a crib and dresser for Emily, and two Adirondack chairs for the porch. He's built a garage alongside the house big enough for his workbench and all of our equipment. But of all these things, I love the bed frame the best, the one he made for me the winter we moved into our house.

The phone rings and I jump to answer, hoping to hear Bell's voice, however crackly, on the other end of the line. But it's Creech, and I try to hide my disappointment.

"How was dinner?"

"Good."

"So, you and Kristen, huh?"

"Why not? She's a nice girl."

Creech is twenty-nine, same as me. Maybe he thinks it's time to settle down.

"First the house, now Kristen. Next you'll be getting a hamster."

He laughs and says, "Speaking of hamsters, you'll never guess who's coming to visit me."

"Bunny?"

"Adam."

Adam is Creech's little brother, middle of the

three Crèches brothers. Creech is the oldest and brother Eric, who's at Syracuse getting an MBA, is the baby. Adam is twenty-six now and not so little anymore. He moved out west, while I was still in college, and I haven't seen him since then. I remember him best as a little kid, skiing hard to keep up with us.

"You are just full of surprises," I say.

"He's visiting the folks in Wells, but he's coming up here next weekend. Why don't you come out with us when he gets here next Friday? We'll go to Lake House for burgers or something."

"I wouldn't want to horn in on your family reunion."

"Horn away, Mallo Cup. Besides, you owe me a dinner."

"Maybe. I'll let you know."

After I hang up, I fight the compulsion to check the website. I do such a good job that I don't check it for a few days. We're pretty busy on the hill, and both Em and I are tired when we get home. Bell will call when he can, I tell myself. Maybe he can't. But the other voice in my head says maybe he doesn't want to.

It's a voice I don't want to hear.

Chapter Ten

The Friday Adam comes to visit, I do morning sweep with Kristen. The two of us check out Approach and the Wilderness, next to the glades, which we probably won't open again until next year. There's not even enough snow there to make ducking the ropes interesting.

I see a rock jutting out mid trail on Approach, hiding under a pack of moguls. Kristen and I mark it. She drills two holes into the snow just over the rock and I plant two flagged poles. We work quietly, though I'm watching her. She's been seeing Creech for a week. She's nothing like the lanky, ivory-girl types Creech usually dates. She's more what might be called cute with a bunch of flyaway dark hair she keeps tucked into a bushy ponytail and a bridge of freckles across a pug nose. She's not very big, a little shorter than I am, maybe about five-two. Kristen seems the kind of girl you might settle in with, and I wonder again if Creech is thinking about settling down.

Kristen catches me looking. "There's another rock by the cut off," I say. "I saw it from the chair."

We ski over to mark off the second rock.

"Mallory?" she says when she finishes drilling. "Are you okay with me dating Creech?"

It's out there now, what I've been thinking about, and I feel myself flush. "Why wouldn't I be?" I try not to sound defensive.

She shrugs. "I don't know. It's just that you and Creech..." She stops as though thinking

86

carefully about what to say next.

"Do you like him?" It's a stupid question, and I feel like I ought to be sent back to junior high for saying it.

"Yeah," she says, "He's great, funny, smart, cute." Now she sounds like she's about thirteen. "I just—" She shrugs again. "Well, I just didn't want there to be any weirdness between us."

"There's nothing to be weird about." But I'm wondering myself. Creech dating someone I know and work with will take some getting used to.

"He says you're going to come with us, to the Lake House with Adam."

Again, I feel something I can't quite put my finger on. Surprise maybe that he's asked Kristen to come. Though why wouldn't he? It shouldn't matter, but somehow it does.

It's a quiet day. Turk has been avoiding me like I have the plague ever since my little tantrum, which is just as well with me. Albie, though, keeps giving me the stink eye. I know he thinks I ought to make nice with Turk because I'm senior to him. I'm still not feeling very charitable towards him. The whole situation has gotten to me enough that I question Coyote about it on an afternoon run.

"Albie thinks I scare him."

I expect Coyote to laugh and tell me that's a load of bull. He does laugh, but then nods thoughtfully.

"Do you think I'm scary?"

"Personally, no," he says "But I can see where Turk might think so. And you've been a little hinky lately."

"A little hinky?" That's three people who have told me I'm spinning out.

I give him a look and he gets defensive. "It's

87

okay, Mallo. I mean, you're fine." He stops and considers. "But you—" he stops again and gets busy lifting the safety bar because we're almost up top.

We ski off, but I catch him. "But what, Coyote?"

"I've never seen you fuck up. Not once. You expect the same from everybody else. That makes you a little..." He stops and searches for a word. "Intimidating."

"Intimidating? Jesus, Coyote."

"You wanted to know," he says and then gives me a no-hard-feelings smile. "I like working with you, if that's what you're wondering." He looks like he wants to say something else, but he doesn't say it. "I'll race you to the top of the Facelift," he says.

He takes off and I'm right on his tail, we're careening down either side of the empty trial, Coyote's whooping and it feels great just letting it fly. I see a line down the center that will beat him for sure, but I think about what he said and I don't take it. He reaches the top of the chair a good five seconds ahead of me. "You're losing your edge, Prescott," he says clicking his tongue.

"I'll get you next time," I tell him.

The end of the day comes quickly. Albie's down at the station waiting after sweep.

"Morning sweep tomorrow," he says to me "I want you to partner with Turk."

I groan and Albie gives me the eye. I know that there's no changing his mind on this one.

He's decided on peace at any cost.

Emily and I go to the Lake House after a quick stop at home to shower and change. I take her into the shower with me and we splash water all over the place, which she likes better than the idea of getting redressed for dinner or getting dressed at all or going out at all.

The restaurant is one of many on Main Street. It's really two restaurants; the upstairs, overlooking the lake, serves Italian food and is pricey. The downstairs, where we go to meet Creech, is a bar with a DJ where burgers and sandwiches are served at big, round, wooden tables.

I spy Creech already seated with Kristen and Adam. Adam gets up when we come over, and he doesn't look at all like the kid I remember. He's filled out. Now he's muscular and tall with a head of dark hair like his brother's and a short five o'clock shadow of a beard. Emily's shy all of a sudden. She's hiding behind me. I think it's because she's not used to adult strangers, and it's weird to think that Creech's little brother is a complete stranger to her.

We order burgers and beers. I get a kiddie burger and juice for Em. Creech has his hand on Kristen's knee and I try hard not to stare at it. Adam tells us about his life out west. He's at Alta in Utah, doing avalanche control. We've had a few avalanches ourselves off the slides on the top of the mountain. They've never been anything serious, but they can happen even in the east if the vertical's right.

Creech talks about his house and says he hopes he and Bell can get it fixed up this summer. He brags how Bell built our house and some of the furniture in it. And he tells Adam all about Alaska. I'm a little surprised at the enthusiastic way Creech talks about the expedition. I didn't think he was excited by it. He knows how I feel about it, so I'm a little hurt at his going on. I don't linger there long.

The volume of music from the DJ climbs a notch and Adam asks me if I want to dance.

"Dance?" I ask, swaying my shoulders to the music. Bell and I dance at home sometimes. When we're alone. It's been ages since I've been out dancing anywhere.

Creech is smiling at me. His eyes have a kind of mischievous twinkle. "Mallo's quite the dancer," he says to Kristen.

"Remember that high school dance?" Adam asks his brother.

"Oh, yeah." Creech's smile has turned into a big grin. "Mallo got up on the refreshment table. Wild woman damn near knocked the punch bowl over with her bumping and grinding."

"As I recall," I say, feeling the heat in my face, "you got up there with me."

"Stevie Winston," says Creech. "God, I took one too many dares from that boy." He puts his arm around Kristen and gives me a nod. "This one never could resist a dare, either."

Emily's taking this all in, her eyes wide as saucers.

"It was a very long time ago," I tell her. I can just imagine her at seventeen, getting up on a table and doing a semi-lewd dance with her boyfriend. The thought is not a comforting one.

"I dare you," Adam whispers in my ear.

"You gonna dance, Mommy?" asks Emily.

I wink at her. "You bet. Somebody's got to show these boys how it's done." I grab Adam's hand. "What are you waiting for?"

The dance floor's about the same size as the table where Creech and I nearly spilled the punch. The DJ's playing "La Vida Loca,"and I start moving around. It feels great, really freeing. Adam churns next to me. Then the music slows into a new rendition of "House of the Rising Sun." Adam takes me by the waist and we do a sort of tango. I catch the look in his eyes as he smiles at me, and I'm reminded again of that long-ago night.

That night, the dance nearly over, Creech and I had gone out back to make out. Adam followed us and found us. Creech jumped him and nearly bashed Adam's head in. Adam had a shiner for a week.

But before the thrashing, there was this moment. Creech's hand had snaked its way under my shirt. He was kissing my neck, and I looked up to see Adam. He had this look in his eyes, like I was lunch and he hadn't eaten in a week. I'd forgotten all about that until just now. Because, just now, he's looking at me the same way.

The music stops again, and I pull away from him. "I think I've had enough."

"I could do this all night," he says and I shake my head and smile. He bows, takes my hand and kisses it. "Thank you, milady."

Creech applauds as we sit down. "Girl, you still got it." He turns to Kristen and asks if she'd like to give it a try and they're off.

"You dance good, Mommy," says Emily.

"She does know how to move," says Adam and there's that look again.

"Come on, baby girl," I say to Emily. "Let's show these guys how it's done." I leave the table with my daughter for the dance floor, before Adam has me for dessert.

I offer to show my house and after dinner we

all drive over to North Elba. Creech has a bottle of red wine in the car. He brings it in and we uncork it to celebrate Adam's trip east. I tell Emily she needs to get ready for bed. She's wired after the restaurant and she's running and hopping around. I get her into her PJ's and notice that I'm stoked from the wine and beer. She fusses when I say bedtime, so I let her stay up a little longer. We finish the wine and I offer to open the bottle I had bought before Bell left.

Emily wants to go to the Daddy Site, and Creech and Kristen say that they'd like a look too. The computer is in a nook upstairs in the sleeping loft and the bed's not made. Tonight I'm not standing on formality, so I tell them to go on up. I give them the URL, though the page is bookmarked, and I'm pretty sure Emily can find it on her own. Adam follows me out to the kitchen when I go to get the wine.

"Nice place," he says, leaning up against the counter.

"I like it."

He smiles at me. "I've always pictured you in a place like this." I hand him the bottle and start digging through the drawer for a corkscrew. "It kind of looks like you."

"Yeah?" I say, distracted by my search.

"Yeah. Only when I imagined your house, I kind of imagined me in it." I stop searching and look up. He's still leaning on the counter smiling at me. He's got hazel eyes, like Creech's. "I had this huge crush on you all through school."

I see the corkscrew, hiding in plain sight on the countertop. Then Adam's hand is on my arm and he's kissing me, right there in my kitchen. And I kiss him back. We neck like a couple of teenagers and then he moves back and I snatch up the corkscrew.

All kinds of thoughts pour through me. Not the least of which is attraction, the one I work to fend off. I clear my throat and I'm getting ready to say something like this isn't a good idea, when I see Creech and Kristen standing with Emily between them on the other side of the room. Now my feelings range more towards guilty panic. How long have they been standing there? By the way they're looking at me, or not looking, I figure I've got some serious explaining to do.

"Mommy, what's a crevasse?" my little girl asks. The question catches me way off guard. I haven't dared to look at Adam. I'm losing my balance enough as it is.

"A crevasse? It's kind of like a hole, sweetie." And then it hits me. Why is she asking about crevasses? I feel another surge of panic and from the look on Creech's face, he can see it as it courses through me.

"Maybe you ought to come see this, Mallo." He looks at me like I'm a horse that might bolt.

"Bell?" The best I can do is whisper his name.

"Bell's okay, Mallory," Kristen says, "Bell's fine." Creech puts his arm around me and we go upstairs. The computer is still on the website. There's a section titled 'Latest News' next to the hyped-up part, which includes a stock photo of Bell and the others. The headline tag says "Tragic Accident on Denali." It's from today's Anchorage paper.

I'm sitting in front of the screen. My hands feel shaky. I sit on them so Em won't know how rattled I am. The cobwebs caused by the beer and wine have faded. I'm stone sober now. Maybe too sober.

"Rod Kirchman," Creech says quietly, "fell into a crevasse early this morning."

I think this can't be. Roddie is one of the best mountaineers around. He's got a wife in New Zealand. He's got two kids. Just last summer, Bell and I went out with Emily to visit them.

I click on the link to the article and page through. Rod mis-stepped, it says. The crevasse was hidden under snow from the previous storm. He fell through the snow cover, over the lip. It doesn't say much else, except he was roped in and the rest of the team pulled him out. It happened near base, but it still took six hours to get him back to camp. From there, he was evacuated by air to Provence hospital in Anchorage, where he is listed in grave condition.

I can't read anymore. I unplug my hand from under me and reach for the mouse to shut the window. Only I can't shut it. Maybe I don't want to. I need to keep staring at the file photo of Kahiltna Glacier that's pasted next to the text. I stare at it as though it will talk to me. I think about Sue Kirchman and her two kids, but I don't let myself stay there for too long, because if I stay too long I won't be able to hold it together.

I feel a hand on my shoulder. I hear Creech saying, let's go downstairs, and I'm aware that they are all there and looking at me: Creech, Kristen, Adam, my little girl. I get up and lead the way down. I sit in the rocker and Emily comes and curls in my lap. I hold her tight.

"Is Daddy in a crevasse?" she asks.

It takes me a minute to find the voice to reassure her. "No, Daddy's fine."

Why didn't he call? Why doesn't he call? Even though I know there's a good chance he can't call,

I'm back to cursing Bell out. Then I amend my thoughts because I'm scared they will fall down on his head, and then something will happen to him. I couldn't live with that. I couldn't face it, if he'd been the one to take the fall.

Almost on cue, the phone rings. It sounds like an alarm, and it jars me. Creech asks if I want him to get it. I shake my head, my phone's right next to the chair. I pick it up.

"Mallory?" Bell's voice is crackling and distant on the other end of the line. I've never been so relieved to hear a voice in my life. "You there?" and I understand that I haven't said anything.

"I'm here." I put Emily down and head back up the stairs. I need to be alone with Bell's voice for a little while. "Where are you?" It's a stupid question, but a part of me is hoping that he'll say he's on a plane heading east.

"Base camp. Roddie had an accident."

I hear the wear in his voice despite the bad connection.

"I saw it posted on the website." I rehash what the article said and ask if Roddie's okay.

Bell doesn't answer for a long time. Finally, he says, "Roddie didn't make it."

His voice breaks and I'm crying right along with him, big sloppy tears that I don't even try to control.

"Mallo?"

"I'm still here."

"God, I miss you so much." And this makes me cry harder. We're silent for a while; I'm cradling the phone.

"Is Emily asleep?

"No," I grab a tissue off the nightstand and call to Emily. "Daddy's on the phone."

She runs up the stairs. I hope she won't pick up on the red eyes. She doesn't seem to notice, her face is one big smile and she grabs the phone from my hand.

"Daddy!" she yells into it. Then there are a few nods, a solemn look at me and some yeses and nos. She hands the phone back over. "Daddy wants to talk to you now." She skips off towards the stairs. Before she goes down, she turns around, runs back to the phone and tells Bell she had pickles for dinner.

"Pickles?" he says, the tension broken for a minute.

I tell him about the Lake House. I'd forgotten about Adam. It really didn't seem all that important anymore. I find myself talking incessantly. I go on about the hill and Turk and Danny's roof and Kristen.

"When will you be home?" I say finally, asking the thing that's most on my mind.

"It might be a little while yet, Mallo."

"A little while?" I had him on the plane tomorrow. Two days, tops. I don't figure on what he says next.

"We're going to do this thing. Dedicate the climb and the ski descent to Rod. It's what he would have wanted."

The door on the world has just slammed shut again.

"You're going to do this thing?" I sound like a stupid child. There's another pause.

"Yeah. We talked about it. We took a vote and decided not to scrap it."

"Took a vote?"

"Yeah, we decided together. It was unanimous. It's a great team, Mallo. We've got to do this. For

Roddie."

Nothing will turn him around. Not my voice. Not Emily's. Not even Roddie Kirchman's death.

I want to yell at him and say he can just stay in Alaska then. I want to slam the phone down. But I don't want to lose the connection. I don't want to hang up because he won't call back.

Chapter Eleven

It takes me a long time to put the phone down and when I do I sit on the bed, everything forgotten except Roddie's accident and Bell continuing the climb. I'm feeling heavy, as though I couldn't move if I wanted to. I don't hear Creech until he's in the room sitting next to me. He just sits and lets me be. I stare out into space and realize it's dark up here. I hadn't switched on the bedside lamp, and the only light is coming up from downstairs.

"Emily fell asleep," Creech says. "Kristen's putting her to bed."

"Roddie Kirchman's dead." I feel the tears well up again. I can't stop them, and so I just let them go.

Creech puts an arm around me and pulls me in close. His sweater is scratchy and smells like dryer sheets. We sit that way for a long time, me wetting his sweater. Kristen calls up the stairs and asks if everything is okay. Creech tells her we'll be right down. He gets me a couple of tissues. I blow my nose and wipe my eyes.

"I don't know if I can go down."

"You want me to send Kristen and Adam home?"

"No. You don't have to stay. I'll be okay." I don't feel okay, and I'm not sure I want to be alone, but I can't hold together enough to deal with anyone.

I hear Creech talking to Kristen and Adam, and then I hear the door shut. Chance barks and I remember I've left him outside. I go downstairs and let him in. He bounds through the door oblivious to my distress.

I hesitate for a moment, then pick up the phone to call Sue. I don't know the number. It's New Zealand. It's not like calling Creech down the street. It's New Zealand and I don't know the number. I don't even know what time it is there. I put the phone down.

There's a drawer under the computer desk. In it is a wide assortment of paper scraps—receipts for climbing gear, several thumbnail sketches of a screen house Bell's been designing for our yard. I find the address book crammed in the back and pull it out. Inside there's a creased paper with "Roddie" printed on it in Bell's sloping hand. Underneath the name are an address and a phone number. I stare at it a minute more, think it has too many digits, and then I pick up the phone again and dial.

A woman answers, I hear kids and dogs in the background. "Sue?"

"No," says the woman. "This is her mum."

"Oh." Not knowing how to proceed, I let the conversation go dead.

"Who's calling?" asks the woman, Sue's mum, after a time.

"It's Mallory. Prescott. I just heard about Roddie." I stop again not trusting my voice.

"Yes. It's been a blow to us all. Sue's off to Alaska, poor dear. Roddie should have stayed home, I told her. He's got children, after all." She stops, but not before I catch the bitter tone of her voice.

"I just wanted to say..." I have to stop a minute because I'm crying again, for Sue and her kids. And for Emily and myself too. "I'm so sorry."

"Yes, well. I'll be sure to tell her you called. Your name again?"

"Mallory." I hang up before she can say anything more.

I go upstairs to change for bed.

"He's got children, after all," Sue's mother's voice keeps leaking into my thoughts, dripping with anger and remorse. "He should have stayed home. He's got children, after all."

I go back down and check on Emily, hoping my own daughter can silence the endless refrain in my head. She stirs when I open the door.

"Mommy?" she mumbles as I pull the covers over her. "We forgot the monster."

"Want to do it now?"

"Can I come sleep in your bed?"

I let her sleep with me, grateful to have her warm little body nested into Bell's side of the bed. Chance turns a few circles at our feet before settling in with a heavy sigh. I watch my little girl sleep, unable to find that kind of peace. I keep thinking about Sue and her two kids and Roddie not coming home to them.

It's late by the time I drift off and I wake up with a headache, too groggy to think straight. I put Chance out on his chain and make coffee, then wake Emily who's even groggier than I am, and the two of us slog through breakfast.

Creech calls and asks if I'm okay.

"Not really."

"Bell will be home soon," he says.

"No, he won't."

I drop Emily off at the nursery. My head is still

throbbing despite the extra strength pain reliever I took. I dread the sweep. The last thing I need today is Turk. I consider telling Albie this, am still considering it when I walk into the station. Everyone goes suddenly quiet, and I feel like they are all staring at me. I get my coffee. Coyote comes over and hands me the cream.

"Kristen told us. About...." he says.

I wave him off. I really don't think I can talk about it. The sympathy is more than I can take.

"We were checking out the website," he says, motioning toward the computer. "Bell's going to go ahead?"

I nod. "Yup."

"Says he's dedicating the climb and ski to his friend. That's really something."

"Man's got a lot of courage," Sully adds. "More than I could muster."

I'm wondering if I understand men at all. I've skied and worked with these guys for years. What I would call stubbornness or obsession, they've labeled courage. Maybe it's me. I don't see it. And I sure as hell don't feel it.

"Where's the Turk?" I make a face. "I've got to partner with him for sweep."

A feeble bout of laughter rolls over from the table.

"He went to get some breakfast," said Sully. "Guess he's not back yet."

Albie walks in and I weigh talking to him against partnering with Turk. Despite my pounding head, I decide I can't afford to be petty. Albie hands out assignments. Turk and I draw the summit down over Cloud Spin.

Turk catches me as I'm snapping on my skis outside the station, a half-eaten sandwich in one hand. The others are already off to the lifts, and I'm in no mood to wait. I start off towards the Facelift quad. I wait up by the chair, and Turk falls in.

"Christ, you can't wait two seconds, Prescott?" he says after we load.

He's stuck the rest of the sandwich in his jacket pocket. I take some small satisfaction in seeing it there. I tell him that his boot's unbuckled, which it is.

He reaches down and snaps it shut. "Wouldn't want to offend you," he says.

"Good."

"God knows I don't want to add any fuel to the 'Get Turk Fired' campaign."

"What are you talking about?"

"Tell me that you didn't talk to Albie about getting rid of me?"

I shake my head at him. I only wish I had that kind of power.

"I saw you," he says. "You and Albie all cozy in the cafeteria. Life would be a lot easier, if you weren't such a bitch." He says the last part under his breath, but I hear it. Clearly, he meant for me to.

I would love to can his ass or toss him off the lift into the trees, but all I do is roll my eyes at him. "You know, you are so full of shit I don't even have a comeback."

"The great and mighty Mallory Prescott," he says. "God help anyone who makes a mistake. Did it ever occur to you that we can't all be fucking perfect? That not all of us have perfect fairy tale lives like you?"

I'm staring at him now. If his comment wasn't so pathetically off the mark, it would be downright funny.

We sweep down Cloud Spin, and there are no new patches of ice or rock that we don't know about. That is, until an unseen rock explodes under my ski and sends it off kilter. I find myself leaning out one legged, the other ski straight out sideways, fighting to keep my balance. Luckily, it's not too steep here. If it were, I would have splatted. But I manage to get both skis back onto the snow and regain my equilibrium. Turk is watching, a big smile pasted on his face.

It's going to be a very long day.

Around noon we come back, and I join Creech, Adam, Kristin, Corky, and Emily for lunch.

"I know what Albie's after," I tell them. "But I think it would be better for me to stay the hell away from Turk."

Creech nods thoughtfully. "I've had kids like that," he says. "They've got to shape or ship. And sometimes they ship. I have no problem with that."

"But you're their coach. They have to listen to you. Turk works with me. I'm not his boss."

"I think he's just jealous, myself," says Adam. He's been giving me funny looks all through lunch. Obviously, I've got more to resolve with him than with Turk.

"The way I see it," he continues. "You're not hard to look at and you're the best skier on the hill."

"Oh, come on,"

"No, Mallo," says Corky. "You can out ski any of us."

Creech looks at me. He's not the skier he was before his accident, but he could give anyone on this hill a run for their money. "True," he says. "You can out ski anyone, except maybe Bell."

Now I know they are just trying to cheer me up.

"Give yourself credit, girl. You still own the NCAA record for Giant Slalom. What's it been—like, seven years?" says Creech.

"Eight," I say. "And big deal."

"It is a big deal. You could do anything. You could do the Denali thing, if you wanted," says Creech. "Maybe you should. Make a name for yourself."

I don't want anything to do with Denali, especially not after yesterday. I pick up my tray and ask Em if she's ready for our after-lunch run. She's got her coat on before I get the sentence out. I help her zip it.

Adam comes after us as we head towards the quad and asks if he can thumb a ride. "Creech didn't mean anything by that," he says. "But he's right."

"It's baloney, Adam," Adam takes the hint. I don't want to talk about Denali, or Bell. Especially not Bell and especially not with Creech's kid brother.

Emily takes a nosedive in the run-off. I'm down next to her before I remember skiing there, and Adam's right behind me. I start checking her over for injuries.

She picks herself up and brushes off her snow pants. "I'm fine, Mom."

I watch her ski off towards the bottom.

Adam looks at me and shakes his head. "She's just like her mother."

He follows me down to the nursery, where I tell Charlotte all about Emily's dixie, much to my little girl's dismay. Charlotte promises to keep an eye out and let me know if there's anything unusual.

"About last night..." Adam starts, when we're out in the corridor.

"Never happened, okay?" I say and walk away from him.

That evening, after I put Emily to bed, I pull the Craigeborne video up on You Tube. It's a homemade video, taken with the phone, from last year when we went to New Zealand to visit Roddie. It's not flashy like the Warren Miller movies Bell made. It's uneven, the camera waves around with wide nauseating swings. The mountains of New Zealand serrate the skyline. The powder's waist deep.

Bell, his skis arching out, makes a smooth S line that tracks behind him like a vapor trail. And I follow in his wake, carving a trail of my own, until there are two hieroglyphs, side by side, indenting the virgin snow. And there's Roddie, sunglasses slipping from the perch of his nose, his dark hair a wild nest, mugging it up for the camera. And now Sue, her belly round with their daughter Wylie, yet to be born. The camera skates and glides. The screen is floating away. I switch it off and close my eyes.

Life seemed so simple then. Will it ever be that way again?

Chapter Twelve

It's Sunday again. A few more weeks and the season will be over. A few more weeks and Bell will be home. We'll help Danny fix his shed. I make a million plans in my head for when Bell is safe in my bed once again.

He doesn't call. I don't really expect him to. Since there's no turning him around, I try to be hopeful.

I ask myself how far he will get today. I have the place names in my head, the ones he climbs to, ascending and descending, back and forth like a birthing process—places with names like Windy Corner, the Orient Express. I don't linger long on Orient Express, remembering the bodies said to litter it like a graveyard of unburied souls. I reassure myself that Roddie's body has been recovered. It occurs to me, though, that for Roddie or for Bell, lying forever along the shoulder of Denali would offer its own kind of solace. There are worse fates, Bell would say, though for myself, at this moment, I can't think of any.

I take a run with Creech in the afternoon. We ride the gondola to Little Whiteface summit. The day is bright, warm enough to make jackets uncomfortable. Clouds scurry along like bunches of sheep and get caught along the stone top of the mountain. We'll be in them soon, a thin white fog.

Creech watches me, quiet. He called twice last night and once this morning. He won't say he's worried, but he acts as though he is. I declined dinner with him and Adam and Kristen after skiing yesterday. I told him I was tired, which wasn't far from the truth, and that Em and I needed some down time. I wondered at the time whether I was avoiding Adam. Now I know I was avoiding all of them.

"He's going to be fine, you know," Creech says.

I want to agree, but Roddie Kirchman has proven there are no guarantees. Creech can see I'm not convinced.

"He's got skill and a great team," he says.

"Skill isn't always enough." Things can change one minute to the next. Look at Creech's accident in Grindlewald. One missed set edge and his dreams were carried away in an ambulance.

"I know that. I've been on the wrong side of luck," says Creech, as though he has read my thoughts. "But I also know that I wouldn't have missed any of those years on the circuit. Even if I had known what was going to happen, I wouldn't have given them up. Even if things had been worse, I wouldn't have changed anything. I think it's the same for Bell. I think you know that."

I tell him I do know. It's true Bell would rather go out like Roddie than not have gone to the mountain at all. Bell could not, and would not, choose a different path. To do so would kill what's best about him. I know this and still it doesn't offer much in the way of comfort. It does not change the fact that Emily and I are here, an eternity of miles away from him, waiting.

The other truth is I am afraid. For myself. For Bell. For our little girl.

The spring of his first try for the rib, Bell left

the last week the hill was open. It was April, and spring had come early to Lake Placid. The mud sucked at our boots when we traveled from the car to the front door of our new cabin. Bell had finished the table, though not the chairs for the great room, and we moved it to a spot near the kitchen island. Honey colored pine, big enough for six; it was missing its appendages.

I was hopeful then. I knew what Bell was doing carried risk. He joked about the movie the Denali park rangers made all the climbers watch. "Worse than those warning movies they show in driver's education," he said. "The old scare-them-straight tactic."

He wasn't worried. He had a good crew. He had Roddie Kirchman. I didn't know Roddie then, but I did know he had a solid reputation as one of the best mountaineers in the world. If anyone could get Bell up and down Denali, it was Roddie. And Bell had more than fair knowledge of mountains himself. He'd dedicated a lifetime to skiing them and that leads to some kind of a contractual agreement. Or so I thought. Denali is not one to keep contracts. The warning movie exists for a reason.

I brought Bell to the airport. My biggest worry in seeing him off was how to get through nearly two months without him. I did tell him to be careful, to which he smiled and said, "I always am."

The next few weeks passed uneventfully. We closed the hill for the season. I got busy seeding a lawn where the grass had been disrupted by construction and putting gravel on the drive, which had become a mud pit. I bought curtains for the kitchen window and flower boxes for the porch rail, though it was far too early to plant anything yet. I visited my dad, who was happy I'd fallen into this new relationship with Bell, and I visited my mom, who was not happy about it.

I counted off the days. Only two more weeks. Only one week. I didn't talk to Bell much. I didn't expect to. Communication is not easy at twenty thousand feet. When the phone rang five days before he was due home, I thought it was Bell, calling from Talkeetna to tell me he was finished early.

The voice on the other end of the phone wasn't Bell's. It was Roddie's. And I knew right away that his calling me via satellite from camp on Kahiltna Glacier could only mean trouble. Despite the upbeat lilt in his voice when he told me there had been a mishap, my heart started beating too fast. I remember it was late afternoon. It was warm and I had opened the windows and the sun was steaming in. I knew guys like Roddie, knew how they downplayed things. A mishap could be anything.

It's been five years, and I can still hear Roddie's voice. "We had to sled him down. Copters won't go that high. We're shipping him off to Anchorage." When I didn't say anything, he added, "Hope I didn't worry you, love."

I lied and told him no. After we hung up, I called the airlines and booked the first flight to Anchorage. I didn't think to call anyone else, didn't think much at all, just packed a few things, and drove to Albany. I don't remember much about the flights, except it was a long ordeal and I was impatient. I don't remember what Anchorage looked like.

They had Bell in a room by the time I got there. He looked like he'd been the loser in a prizefight. One eye was swollen shut, one hand

109

bandaged because of frostbite on two fingers.

He looked up when I came in. "Mallory," he said, as though I were some kind of apparition. "Jesus, Mallory, honey, what are you doing here?"

"Thought I'd drop by for a visit,"

I was trying at the time to unhinge an awful fear, the awful thought of Bell as fallible, as vulnerable. It sat in my head, reinforced by tape and bandages and the blistering on his face. It sat there and I couldn't shake it. It still sits there, this heavy pulsing gravitational thought.

When I think of Bell on Denali, this is the picture I get. Bell vulnerable. Bell fallible.

I beg off beers and pizza again with Kristen and Creech, alone this time because Adam's gone to spend the day in Wells. When we get home after work, Em gets out of the Jeep and runs to the porch. It's exceptionally quiet. Usually, the cut of the car engine is met by the steady bark and howl of Chance out on his chain by the doghouse. Chance likes to climb on his shelter, sit on the apex of the roof, and howl at the peaks, which echo back his voice in an uncanny imitation. He howls back at the echo, and plaintive cries from either side begin to ricochet back and forth. For this reason, I don't leave him out at night.

Emily notices the quiet, too and runs around back calling for the dog. She comes back, her mouth pursed in a worried frown. "He's not there," she says.

I walk back with her. There's a funnel hole where Chance has excavated the chain post, sharp and deep as though it were a carrot he dug out of the ground. I squint out towards the woods, a long shadow, paw prints, and the snake-like imprint of a chain shimmer in a track towards the brook. I move to the wood's edge into the deep pine shadows and call. My echo answers.

My little girl's eyes fill with tears. I call again, my echo falls to quiet. Even the creek, still frozen, has no intoxicated babble. The track of chain, itself an echo, disappears into the thick of trees.

A wind blows up and scatters the pines, restlessness combing the branches. It's gotten too dark to run into the woods. I turn on the porch light, travel down as far as the creek, and call again. Still nothing.

I'm worried about the chain; Chance could wind it around a tree. He could choke. My imagination conjures up images I'd rather it didn't. I take Emily inside. She's crying hard now, sobbing in the way children are allowed to and adults aren't. "You have to do something, Mommy."

"We'll look down along the road," I tell her, not because I think we'll find him but because it's something to do and it's better than fretting here at home.

We climb back into the Jeep and jostle along, farther down the dirt road on which we live. Beyond the cabin, the road narrows until, about three miles down, it ends altogether at a junction with the creek. It's almost fully dark now; the trees have turned to edgy shadows stirred by the wind. Emily leans from her booster seat in the back and presses her small hands to the window.

"Over there!"

I stop the car and turn the flashlight I've brought to where she's pointing. Nothing. No paw prints. No chain. We drive to the end of the road, turn around and bump all five miles back to the main road. I drive slowly, stopping every mile or so to get out and search with the flashlight and call. We turn back towards the cabin. Emily begs for one more pass, so I drive past our driveway down the deserted road to the end.

"Oh, where is he?" cries my little girl, breaking my heart.

"Maybe he came home." We drive back to the cabin. Creech's truck is in the driveway. Thank goodness, he can help us look. I park next to it, and Adam, not Creech, pops out from driver's side of the cab.

He comes towards us, his face washed in the shadow by the porch light. "Hey Emily," he says, but she's crying too hard to take note.

"Our dog's gone missing." I have a fair idea of why he's here, and I need to let him know this is not the time for that discussion. I'm almost glad for the excuse, because I really don't want to talk with him. "Wait with Em on the porch, will you?"

Before either one of them can protest, I take the flashlight and head back down toward the creek, following the snaky trail Chance's chain has left in the snow. I travel several hundred yards beyond the creek. It's too dark to see anything except the silvery outline of trees in the narrow funnel of the flashlight's beam. Snow crunches loudly underfoot. I stop a minute, and hear Emily calling me. The dog's path would take me farther west, but I turn and head towards my daughter's voice.

The blue flashers are evident even from the backyard. I run towards them, my flashlight's beam dancing in circles in the snow in front of me. Emily and Adam are standing next to a state police car. The driver's door is open and a trooper has gotten

112

out. I hear a bark and there's Chance, sitting in the back of the squad car like a two-bit hood.

The trooper turns and shuts his door when he hears me, his hat casting an ominous mask over his eyes. Chance is jumping up on the window, running back and forth on the seat looking for a way out. The broken chain is in the trooper's hand. "You folks are going to need a better hook for this guy." He hands the chain to Adam.

Emily has stopped crying. She looks at the trooper with a sort of wide-eyed amazement. I don't quite know what to say myself. I have this ludicrous thought that Chance is going to get carted off to jail. Adam pipes in, as though Chance were his dog and thanks the trooper for finding him." We were worried," he says. As though there were a 'we.'

"Why don't I put him in the house?" I say. Chance's paws are churning against the window glass making a disturbing scratchy sound. The trooper comes around and opens the door. I grab Chance by the collar. He's wagging and wiggling, and I have to anchor my feet and dig my fingers deep into his fur to keep hold of him. I tell Emily to lead the way. As I figured, Chance is anxious to follow and drags me after him towards the house. I put him in Emily's room. He starts whining and pawing at the door. I reassure Emily, who is whining outside the door, that it's only for a few minutes, just until we get things settled. Though I'm feeling so unsettled myself that I'm not sure this will be any time soon.

The trooper's still standing in the drive talking to Adam. "As I was telling your husband, ma'am...." he says. The mistaken identity jolts me, though I don't say anything to correct it. "We found the dog up at your neighbor's. A Mr. Gremler. He called when the dog got into his chicken coop. He thought it was a coyote and was ready to shoot, but then he saw the tags. He says he knows the dog, and this isn't the first time it's happened."

Earl Gremler owns a farm a half a mile through the woods from our cabin. He's called us twice because Chance has escaped and gone over there. Last time Mr. Gremler was pretty mad. Bell fielded the call. Seems Chance got into the Gremler's cow pasture and was riding one of the cows. I thought at the time Gremler had quite an imagination. Chance is excitable, but he would never hurt anyone. He's really just a big old baby. But this time, the trooper was called, and now a man in uniform is telling me that my dog is a menace.

"I saw the destruction, ma'am. Your dog killed two of Mr. Gremler's chickens. He says if you pay for damages, he won't press charges. He also says if it happens again, he will shoot the dog."

I take an anxious glance towards the porch to reassure myself Emily is out of earshot.

"He can't do that," I say, realizing the horror I'm feeling at the picture in my head, a picture of Chance lying still as a rug, an immobile pile of fur.

"He'd be within his rights, ma'am, if there's destruction of property or threat to himself."

"Chance would never attack anyone. That's ridiculous." I'm near tears.

The trooper looks troubled. "I don't doubt that. He seems a friendly enough guy. Gremler as much as admitted the dog came over to him wagging his tail, when he surprised him in the coop. Probably what kept him from getting himself shot this time." His eyes flash back to Adam. "Be a shame if anything happened to him. He's a beautiful animal.

My advice is, keep him restrained better."

I thank him, not feeling at all grateful in light of what he's just told me. He gets back into his car and backs out of the drive, the blue flashers still turning until he switches them off, and we are thrown into a darkness stained only by the porch light.

"Mommy," my little girl calls from the porch. "They won't hurt Chance, will they?" She's crying again. I go to her and put my hands to her shoulders. Adam crunches up the drive behind me.

"Let's go in," I tell her. "We'll close the doors and then we can let Chance out of your room." I close the front door behind Adam. "Okay, all shut. You can let him out."

"But is it locked, Mommy?" We have never once locked the front door of our house. But she's looking at me with such earnestness that I slide the lock shut.

Emily lets the dog out and he circles her, wagging his tail and then bounds over to me and licks my hand. If dogs could smile, this one is doing it now. Trying to charm the socks off us.

Emily takes his muzzle in her hands and, like a stern mother, tells him that he was a bad doggie to run off like that. The dog whimpers and sits. Willing, it seems, to be scolded.

I ask Adam to stay for dinner, given that I don't think I have a choice. My daughter will kill me if I attempt to open a door or even a window. There's not much to eat in the house. Tomorrow's Monday and I plan on going shopping before heading over to see Danny—or check up on him, as he likes to say. I heat a frozen pizza and find some carrot sticks that aren't too shriveled to go with it. I give Em the last of the milk and pour tap water for

Adam and me.

At bedtime, Emily asks if Chance can stay with her and though he usually finds a spot in the great room or up in the loft, he seems more than happy to hop up on Emily's bed and wind himself into a cozy nest beside her. By the time I finish reading her a story, they are both asleep, Em with an arm slung around Chance's furry neck, and Chance giving out little snorts of air, as though he's dreaming of chasing chickens.

Chapter Thirteen

I find Adam in the kitchen rummaging through the cupboards, looking for the world like he owns the place. His familiarity and the fact that he's still here makes me uncomfortable.

I cross my arms. "What do you think you're doing?"

"Looking for that bottle of wine we never drank," he says, without stopping his search.

I reach up and shut the cabinet door. I thought I'd made myself clear yesterday but apparently not.

He starts searching through the cupboard where I stashed the bottle. "Aha!" He retrieves the bottle from the cabinet and puts it on the counter.

I reach the corkscrew before he does. "What are you doing?"

"I was going to open the wine," he says. "You've had a rough day. You could use some."

I put the corkscrew back in the drawer and the wine back in the cupboard. "I don't want to drink wine right now, Adam. I'm tired. You need to go home."

He looks at me. His eyes are the color of hemlock. "I don't think you really want me to go home."

I close my eyes, trying hard to hold on to the little bit of sanity I have left. I'm trying to remember how well I know this guy. In high school, I spent more time at his house than at my own. The Crèches brothers took me in as a kind of honorary

117

sister. It was better at the Crèches than at my own house. My parents were engaged in an endless cold war silence—my mother with her hate of the place my father had dragged her to and my father forced into an icy defense of the choices he made. At Creech's house, there was always a kind of warmth, his dad plopping an extra burger onto the grill for me without my asking, his mom handing me a paring knife to cut tomatoes into the salad.

Adam was a kid then, thirteen to my sixteen, to Creech's sixteen. He's twice that age now, twice the experience, and I no longer know how to measure him.

He puts a hand to my arm, begins rubbing. "I don't want to go yet."

"I told you," I wonder if I really want him gone.

"I know what you said, Mallory. And I know things haven't been easy for you. Anyone with eyes can see that."

I wish he would stop. This line of conversation is not one I want to take. I won't be able to crunch it down. I won't be able to swallow.

He moves his hand to my face, runs his fingers along my cheek, then pulls it back. "I saw your dad today," he says, changing the subject. "They plan on closing after this weekend. Doesn't pay to stay open now that the school programs are done."

My dad and John Crèches live and die by the school programs at the elementary and high schools in the area to which they offer ski-and-learn packages. They advertise themselves as a small family-oriented operation. It works for them. They know they can't compete head on with big ski corporations and they can't stay in business without a niche.

"Eric's going into the business with them,"

Adam tells me. "He graduates in May. My dad says he knows more than God now."

I smile at this. Eric always did think that he was smarter than God, even when he was eight. His smarts were the only defense he had against two older brothers.

"A smile," says Adam, and I pull myself back into my carapace.

He starts singing 'smile a little smile for me, Mallory,' making his voice go high, and I can't help but smirk at him.

"You always were a crazy little kid," I tell him.

I'm remembering him at ten, climbing to the top of the tallest pine in the Crèches yard. His brothers had laid two mattresses under the trunk and we were all taking bets if Adam would make the jump. I can still see him, lanky arms and legs, crawling out on an upper branch. He jumped out past the branches, grabbed his knees and turned a full somersault in the air before landing on his back hard enough to pop springs. It must have hurt like hell, but he just got up, smiled, and gave us all a bow.

"I'm not a little kid anymore."

And then I'm in his arms again, a rehash of what happened the other day, and he's kissing me again. My resolve, what little there is left of it, jumps out of that long ago tree and tumbles head over heels towards the ground.

His lips are on my neck, my collarbone. I'm thinking I should stop him, and I'm thinking I don't want to. I press my hands into the back of his neck. His hair is soft where it meets the collar of his shirt. I find it hard to catch my breath.

I push him back without much conviction. I go to the cabinet and retrieve the wine. "I think I've changed my mind."

"I knew you would." He grabs the corkscrew, takes the wine from me, and kisses my neck.

"We drink the wine and we talk," I say. "We just talk."

His hand combs through my hair.

"Just talk," I say again, though I don't sound like I mean it even to myself.

"Just talk," he says.

I sit in the rocker and make him sit on the couch. Six feet of distance; I hope it's enough.

"It was great being home again," he says "Weird, but great."

I nod my head. I've often felt the same about visiting Ridge Run. "I haven't been down there all winter. My dad and I talk on the phone once in a while, but both of us have been pretty busy and it's been a while since I've spoken to him."

"I'm thinking about moving back," he says. "Going into partnership with Eric. He's going to need help running the place."

"He'll have lots of help. My dad and yours know what they're doing."

"My dad and yours aren't going to want to hang around forever. My folks are talking about retiring in a couple of years. About spending the winter in Florida. Can you imagine my dad in white shoes and a matching white belt? Or my mom in a lavender tracksuit?"

"No."

We both laugh. I take another sip of wine.

"What about you?" he asks.

"What about me?"

"You ever consider moving back? Your dad would love that."

It's true. My dad would like my going into the

business. We get on great when we're together. Cut from the same cloth, my mom would say. But it's hard to go home again once you've been away. You can't just pretend you're still sixteen and nothing has changed.

"I don't think I could do that." My glass is empty. "More wine?" His glass is empty, too.

"Sure."

"I'll get it."

He follows me into the kitchen. "I know," he says when I give him a questioning look. "Just talk."

I feel lightheaded after the glass of Chardonnay. I pour myself another glass and pour another for Adam.

The phone rings. It's Creech checking to see if I'm okay again. I'm not sure what to tell him. I'm not okay, not really. I tell him about Chance. I don't tell him about Adam, not even when he says that his brother's left him stranded and that he may have to bum a ride tomorrow.

"What about Kristen?"

"What, Prescott, you can't find it in your heart to give me a lift?" He pauses. "Kristen isn't such a good idea right now."

"You want to talk about it?" I turn my back on Adam, making him disappear.

"Not much to talk about. Things didn't work out. It happens." Creech's voice sounds tired. "Shit. Tomorrow's Monday, isn't it?"

"Don't sweat it. I'll get you to the hill."

Adam is sitting on the stool by the kitchen island, one leg hooked over the rung, looking as though he's been sitting there most of his life waiting for me to notice him. "My brother?" he asks when I hang up the phone.

"He needs his truck back."

"He doesn't know where his truck is, though, does he?" When I don't answer, he walks over to me and puts his lips to my hair.

"What is it you want from me, Adam?"

"You know the answer to that question." He lifts my chin with his fingers, kisses me lightly on the lips. "It's the same thing you want."

"You don't know what I want."

I walk away from him, retrieve the wine I left on the counter, and take a deep sip. "It's not that easy. I have responsibilities. Commitments." The last word come out sideways, like it's too big for my mouth.

"That's not how I see it," he says, stepping in closer. He brushes his hand through my hair. "You're a free agent, Mallory. You don't owe anyone anything."

I like the sound of this despite myself. I hate having to stay here and play the grownup, while Bell plays chicken with Denali. I hate having to deal with Chance. I hate being left alone to parent Emily. I want to be free of it. And next to me, here in my kitchen, is this very attractive man who wants me. I can't help being attracted back. I swallow deep.

He pulls his arms around my waist, draws me in. He kisses my neck again, murmurs that I'm so pretty. I know it's a line, but I don't care. My head is spinning, and it's not just the wine.

He kisses me hard, his tongue lunges into my mouth and I'm pressed up against the counter. Adam's hand roams over my breast. "Want to go upstairs?" he whispers into my ear.

Upstairs flashes through my brain. The loft is a mess; I hadn't bothered to make the bed. The bed

122

where Bell and I sleep. The bed with the headboard Bell made for me. I think of Bell's hands, taking days and weeks to fashion the branches together.

Adam's hands stroke my back, insistent and full of fire. I know whose hands I want and they are not Adam's.

I gasp, which Adam misinterprets as a statement of passion. "Mallo," he says, "God Mallo, you are so beautiful."

I put the flat of my hands against his chest and give him a gentle push. He looks into my eyes, a wild, slightly wicked look that changes when he catches the look in mine. He breathes in short and ragged spurts like a man who's been in the ring and wants to keep fighting though the bell has rung. I bite my lip, knowing I have to say something.

"I can't."

He pulls his hands through his hair.

"I'm sorry, but I can't. You were wrong about the free agent thing. I'm not a free agent."

He strokes my hair. "Maybe I can make you forget about those so-called commitments."

I push his hand away, as angry with myself as I am with him.

"You don't have to make it so hard, you know," he says. "It's easy."

"It's not easy. And this isn't what I want."

"If it wasn't what you wanted, you wouldn't have kissed me back just now."

"Damn it, Adam. Go home. Please."

"So you can go upstairs alone and brood over a man who won't marry you? Or is it Creech you're still brooding over?"

I shove him hard. He's a lot bigger than me, but I'm a lot angrier. He stumbles, nearly falls.

"Out, now." I say, barely controlling my voice.

"Jesus, you work pretty damn hard at that tough-girl shit, don't you? Keep it up long enough, and you'll turn into a bitch."

I want to scream at him. I'm a mess, and I'm falling apart and he can't see it. One thing is certain—I'm not about to roll over for him. I'm not about to expose my underbelly.

He slams the front door behind him. I wait until I hear the truck pitch gravel in the drive, and I throw his half-empty wine glass at the door. It shatters into the same number of pieces as my heart.

I'm out and out weeping now—for myself and Bell and Roddie. I'm even crying for Chance. I want Bell here. I want him in our bed. I want him to tell me I'm not so tough. I'd expose all that vulnerable flesh to him. I know he'd take care with it.

Chapter Fourteen

I fall asleep still dressed and wake up feeling purged. It's just past midnight and Chance, the old scoundrel, has found his way to the foot of my bed. He raises his head when I get up, looks contrite as though he's waiting for my forgiveness.

I give him a scratch behind the ears, and he lets out a long low sigh. "What am I going to do with you?" I ask him. He doesn't have any answers, but he closes his eyes to the scratching and I wish that I could be so easily contented.

I go downstairs. The lights are still on, there's glass all over the threshold. I sweep up the remnants and throw them away. A distance of hours and sleep has made me reprimand myself. What was I thinking, letting him kiss me like that? And I think again about the way we left it. Adam storming out after disagreeable words that remind me of Turk's disagreeable words. And at this late hour, when everything seems to run toward the negative, I'm wondering why it is Bell and I never got married.

A few weeks after he found out about Emily, Bell did ask me. He said, "I think we should get married." Casually, almost in passing, the way he might have said, "I think we should have hamburgers for dinner."

I'm not sentimental. I didn't expect he would get down on one knee and present me with a solitaire diamond. What I did want was a pledge. I wanted an "I love you." I wanted him to want to marry me. Not because I was pregnant and he felt obligated, but because he wanted to. Since that time, when I told him no, the word marriage hasn't been spoken between us. It's as though it's been expunged from our vocabularies. Neither of us wanted to say it again, because it held too much. A disaster of a word, one we were better off without.

Still, I think, if Bell really loved me...I catch myself. What then? I can finish the sentence a hundred different ways. And because it's very late and I'm very alone, each time I think about the love he does offer, it comes up short. It's not enough.

I manage to get back to sleep and I get up at six, happy to have a reason not to be in bed anymore. I keep busy all morning, so that I don't have to think too hard. There's plenty to do. Monday's my only day off, and even when Bell's home the day is packed with chores. Today I'm on a tear: I sort laundry and throw a load into the washer, scrub the bathtub, and dust the furniture. When Emily gets up, I scramble the few eggs we have left. I make a list for the market and call Danny to let him know what time we'll be by.

Danny doesn't have a cell phone or even an answering machine. His phone is a black rotary dial model that's old enough to be a museum piece. Danny balks at the idea of changing it. He would no more own a smart phone or a computer than he would leave his cabin and take an apartment in a condo complex. He answers after twelve rings, just as I'm about to hang up. I ask him if he wants me to pick up anything at the store and he gives me his list. As always, I hear the reluctance in his voice. As always I ignore it. I add eggs and soap to the list, because I'm pretty sure he's forgotten them. I don't tell him about Roddie. It's not the kind of thing you want to say over the phone, unless it can't be helped. I do tell him about Chance, though, and I worry aloud about what I'm going to do.

"Bring him here," says Danny. "I can take him for a while".

This solution seems heaven sent. Chance loves being out at Danny's and gets on great with his dogs. Danny lives a long way from the Gremler's, or any farm, for that matter. Far enough to keep Chance from getting into trouble.

"That would be really good, if you're sure it's okay," I tell him.

"What's not okay about it? He's a good dog. Keep me and the girls company." I smile that Danny refers to his dogs as 'the girls'.

After I hang up, I tell Emily that Chance is going to go live with Danny for a while. She doesn't see this as a wonderful solution. She runs over to the dog and clamps her arms around his neck. Chance wouldn't accept this kind of abuse from anyone but Emily. For Emily, he stands there and throws me an exasperated look. "But Mommy, he's our dog."

"It's only for a little while, sweetie."

"But why? Why can't he stay here?" She clutches him so hard that he breaks the hold and scampers off. "Oh, Chance," she calls after him, as though he's disappointed her too.

"It's only for a little while. Until Daddy gets home. We go up to Gramps every week and you can visit him."

She frowns at me, clearly not buying my argument.

"It's only for a little while," I repeat. "It's the best thing for Chance right now. He can run around and he doesn't have to be chained."

I don't mention Gremler's threat. It would frighten her. It frightens me.

"He's our dog, Mommy. Daddy wouldn't like it."

I'm losing patience. "Daddy's not here. Chance is going up to Gramps, and I don't want to hear any more about it."

She stomps off and flings herself on her bed. I threaten her into her coat for our trip to Danny's. It's warmed up. Warm enough, almost, for spring jackets. My mind wanders back to Denali. No spring jackets there. It's never warm. And I wonder if Bell needs to freeze me out. If he needs to be rid of me every once in a while. And if, maybe, he really doesn't want me around at all.

Emily wants to bring Chance into the market and I have to put my foot down again. She doesn't talk to me the whole shopping trip. I try to make amends by letting her choose a box of cookies, but this is a paltry peace offering and she knows it. She brushes Chance's thick pelt all the way up to Danny's. "Poor Chancey," she says, "I love you, poor Chancey," in a way that breaks my heart and makes me want to throttle her at the same time.

Chance is more than happy in Danny's yard. He and Danny's lab, Ella, are romping around. Emily's in the fray. She's laughing and for the moment she's forgotten her grudge.

"Sure he's not going to be too much trouble?" I ask Danny.

"Hell, no. I'm old, girl, not dead. I still got it in me to care for the pup."

I don't doubt that. Danny's skinny skis are propped up against the side of the cabin. He's up with the sun every morning, on the trail in the woods behind his house. "Taking the girls for a stroll," he calls it. He'll often ski six or seven miles at a rip. A long stroll. Chance is going to like it here.

I heat water for coffee. Danny has an old drip pot that you have to pour hot water into. If you ask, he'll tell you it's worked for a lot of years and it's not about to stop working. I call out to Emily and ask if she wants cocoa. She tells me no thank you. The way she says it lets me hope she really is over her disappointment, Though I don't look forward to leaving without the dog.

"So, how's tricks?" Danny asks when I pour him a cup of coffee, which always seems to come out like sludge when I make it, though he doesn't complain.

I don't answer him right away, because the truth is that tricks aren't so good.

"Roddie Kirchman had an accident," I tell him.

Danny only met Roddie once, when he came to visit us the spring after Emily was born. Roddie had just finished a climb in the Sawteeth. Before he left Alaska, he bought a puppy for us. I can still see him standing at our door, a broad smile on his freckled face, a tiny parcel of fur tucked under his arm.

Chance was the cutest thing you'd ever want to see. He had big blue eyes, not unlike Bell's. He whimpered the first night we had him, and Bell ended up putting him into bed with us. Emily was still in the cradle next to our bed, and after her middle-of-the-night feeding, I'd bring her into bed with us too. So there we were—me, Bell, our baby, and our puppy. I remember thinking how warm it all felt. How cozy.

Roddie bunked in what became Emily's room. He snored, loud enough that Bell and I could hear him upstairs.

I rolled over restless and Bell put his hand to my arm. "He keeping you awake?"

"He's a little loud. How do you put up with him in a tent?"

"Ear plugs," he said.

And though it wasn't particularly funny, we laughed over this until I had tears running down my cheeks. Now Emily has her own room, the dog's staying with Danny, and Roddie's not keeping anyone awake at night. Except maybe Sue. I wonder how well she's sleeping. If she's sleeping at all.

Danny studies me, blue eyes in a leather pouch of a face, and I have to tell him the rest.

"He didn't make it," I say, echoing Bell's words on the phone.

"Oh, that's too bad."

You can see he means it. These are the only words he has to pin to tragedy. I imagine him saying, "That's too bad," when Bell's mom died or when his own wife died. That's too bad about covers it. It is. Too very bad to contemplate.

"Bell's going to stay and finish. He's dedicating the climb to Roddie," I say. The telling leaves a bad taste in my mouth. I take a swig of coffee.

I can see that Danny is gauging what to say. He knows I won't like his opinion, though I already know what it is.

"It's only right," he says. And he waits, because he knows that I'll want to counter this. When I don't, he says "But you don't like it," and opens the door for my argument.

I get up and look out the window. Emily is sitting in the snow, one hand petting Chance's thick fur, the other scratching Ella's ears. The dogs sit like guardians on either side of her.

"I want him here," I say to Danny.

"He'll be back soon enough. He's like that dog. He knows where his house is."

"Does he? I mean, what are we really? Just a couple of people who happen to live together."

"You don't believe that, do you, girl?" The question is rhetorical, and I don't answer. Danny purses his lips as though he wants to say something but won't. "You could change it if you wanted," he says finally.

"Bell doesn't want to change it. He's happy with things the way they are."

"And you're not?"

I shrug. "It's okay, I guess."

"Call me old fashioned, but I always thought the two of you ought to get hitched."

"So Bell can make an honest woman of me?" I say, going for a laugh that I don't get.

"Woman's got to be willing." He gets up and starts rummaging through the cupboard. "Late for lunch," he says, holding up a can of soup in each hand. "What kind do you think Emily will like— chicken noodle or alphabet?"

"Alphabet. And what do you mean about willing?"

He hands me the soup. "You want crackers?"

"Danny."

"You're not going to let it slide, are you?"

I cross my arms and he sits down.

"I'm telling tales out of school. I wouldn't tell you at all, except"—and here he gives me a pointed stare that is so much like Bell's that it makes me swallow hard—"I think you need to hear it."

Chapter Fifteen

I'm hoping this isn't another of Danny's stories, the squirrelly ones that don't relate to anything without an explanation. He usually tells these with a twinkle in his eye, to let you know he knows they're off the mark and he's an old man so he can get away with telling stories that don't have a point. But his eyes aren't twinkling now. He's dead serious.

"PD was never much for tears," he begins. "When he was fourteen or so, he fell off the roof. Damned fool thing to climb up there in the first place. He broke his wrist. They didn't give him pain medication at the hospital. That sucker must have throbbed something awful, and the kid didn't say boo about it. But he had this look about him, like the world was all wrong and backwards. I'd seen that look on him the weeks after his mama died. And I'd seen it when he come over to tell me he'd gotten you into trouble, with Emily on the way, and you said no when he asked to make it right." Danny takes a sip of his coffee.

I open the soup can, because I need something to do. My telling Bell 'no' when he suggested we get married hadn't sat well with him, but I really thought he'd only asked out of some misplaced sense of honor.

"Make it right," I tell Danny. "I didn't want him to feel he had to make it right."

"You made yourself pretty clear. He came here out of the blue that day. Said he'd been driving around. He was real out-of-sorts. And you know me. I don't like to mince my words. So I ask him straight out if you and he'd had a fight.

"She's pregnant. She won't marry me," he said, and there was that look. He said he wanted to do it right, wanted to do it better than his father had done by him."

Danny looked at me hard enough that I had to look away.

"I stood up for you, girl. Said maybe being in the family way wasn't enough for you. I asked him right out if he loved you, and his look changed. He looked at me like I'd gone and stared at the sun too long and lost my brains. "Course I love her," he said. "She's the best damned thing that ever happened to me.""

I've sat down again. The soup is still in the can sitting next to the can opener and an empty pot.

"The both of you have always been stubborn as a pack of mules. And if you think for a second that boy don't want to marry you, you're a bigger fool than I credit you for."

I remember that night all too well. I hated that Bell had walked out. I worried he wouldn't be back and breathed a sigh of relief when I heard his Jeep churn the gravel in our drive. He dropped his keys on the counter when he came in.

"We'll do whatever you want," he said, and he went upstairs and didn't say anything else.

Emily doesn't want to leave when it's time to go home. I'm not surprised, but I was hoping I could sell her on how happy Chance is at Danny's. He's more than willing to let us go, trotting off with Ella as soon as we pull out of the drive. This isn't comforting. It only adds insult to injury. Em's crying, I can hear her snuffling in the backseat. Though she's being quiet about it, it's killing me. When I let her out of the car seat when we get home, she turns away from me. She's been wiping her nose on her sleeve and her shirt needs changing, but I don't have the heart to hassle her just now. She sits on the porch steps while I lug the groceries in. She usually likes to help, she's at that age where helping still seems like fun, and she can usually be counted on to carry in a bag or two. Today, she turns her head away every time I walk by. I let her sit while I put things away. I figure she needs space and that she'll come around soon enough.

She needs space, just like her father. Bell always chooses solitude when things go wrong. I think back to what Danny told me and tell myself that nothing is wrong. It's been five years since all that happened, and in those five years we've had good times and bad, but I've never considered leaving.

Has Bell? He's gone off often enough. With his business, he's gone for a week or two at a time, five or six times a winter. And then there's climbing. He's been everywhere from Mt. Blanc to Mt. Rainer. He and Roddie even went to the Himalayas once, though bad weather cancelled the expedition. Three trips up Denali. The second one almost fatal, so of course he repeats it. It's as though he needs to tempt fate. He has to push the envelope. Bell's always been that way. He was that way long before we met. And I could spend two lifetimes thinking up reasons why and not come up with a satisfying answer.

It's cold out there, and near dinnertime, and I

figured Emily should have come in on her own by now. She's still on the porch when I peek out the window, elbows on knees, head resting on her hands, staring off towards Tawahus, which is quickly fading in the encroaching darkness. I go out and sit next to her, hugging my own knees, and we sit there in silence until it's too dark to see much at all.

"I'm sorry you're so sad about Chance," I say.

She nods. In the dark, lighted only by the house lights, she looks so small and vulnerable I have to resist the urge to put both my arms around her. She's not ready yet. My hugging her would only reopen the wound she's trying so hard to close.

"I'm going to miss him too." She nods again and pulls herself a little closer to me. I put one arm around her and she nuzzles into me, her little head warm despite the cold night air.

"I miss Daddy," she says.

I feel a knot crawl up in my throat, my own misting filling my eyes.

It's so quiet. Something I don't notice so often because I've grown used to it. Out here, a distance separating the nearest neighbor, there is a silence that falls on winter evenings. If you listen into the quietude, you can hear the brook breaking free of its icy skin, the last of the snow shedding from the hemlocks. The quiet surrounds us as we sit there, Em and I, and we take it in for a little while until she lifts her head and asks if we can call her Daddy.

"No, sweetie. There's no way to get in touch with him." For a minute I think she might be angry with me again, but she takes this in stride. "We could go to the Daddy Site," I offer. "See what's up."

This cheers her, and we head upstairs to have

a look. Not much has changed since I last looked, but the weather report from Talkeetna, a postage stamp on the side of the page, has a snow icon. I click it.

"The extended forecast calls for heavy snow in the Denali Park area," it says. This is not news I want to read and I don't report it to Emily. I choose instead to point out again the route that Bell will take, over Kahiltna Glacier, around the Windy Corner, to the West Rib, which stands off of Denali's massive South Peak like a stony side porch. She traces her finger over the red line marking the trail on the map. I try to calm myself over the weather.

Bell's not stupid, I tell myself. He won't go up in dismal weather. This doesn't work because he's probably already well on his way, somewhere around eighteen thousand feet. I try a different tack. It's an extended forecast. The weather is hard to predict five days in advance. The weather on Denali, like the weather in our own mountains, is a fickle thing. Surprise storms are not uncommon. Neither are predicted storms that never materialize or never measure up to their potential. I keep this in mind. Five days is a long time to predict the weather. There's a good chance the forecast is off.

I tell Emily she can choose dinner and then hope I haven't made a mistake. She may well ask for ice cream sandwiches and chips, and then I'll have to rescind my offer.

"Burgers and carrots. That's Daddy's favorite." She smiles at me in a way that makes my heart too tender to bear.

We've been having burgers a lot lately. I wonder if there's some unconscious connection, if I'm trying to draw Bell close. Emily's mood has changed. She's content to look at the pictures on the web site and then go downstairs for dinner. She helps out by getting out American cheese for her burger and opening a bun on her plate. I hand her a plate. "Put some carrot sticks on it."

She does. "I like them on dishes better than on the plate. Much nicer this way," she says, sounding amusingly grown-up.

We hear a car door slam as we sit down to eat. I hope against hope it's not Adam come back for round two. I don't think I can stand any more drama in my life. After last night, I have my doubts that he'll show up any time soon. It's not Adam at any rate—it's Creech. I'm not so sure I want to see him after what happened last night either.

I offer to make him a burger, but he says he's already eaten. He does take the glass of milk that Emily offers him. "It's good for you," she says, making both of us smile.

"You forgot me this morning," he says.

A little flag goes up and I'm feeling guilty. About this morning and last night.

"It's okay," he continues. "Adam blew in late, so I've got my wheels back."

"Oh," I say, and he gives me a funny look that leaves me wondering how much he knows.

If he knows anything, he's not letting on. He talks about work, about his season being almost over. "Adam's leaving tomorrow," he says.

This catches me unawares. I thought he'd stay out the week, maybe longer.

"Really? He's going back to Alta?"

"You sound surprised."

"I don't know. I thought maybe he'd stay on a while."

"Yeah, I thought so too. Before he went to

Wells yesterday, he was talking about maybe moving back for good. Then this morning, he says he's going out west. Needs to get back to work, he says."

Emily's been busy eating and now that she's polished off her burger, she's looking at us intently. "Mommy, Adam won't take Chance, will he?"

"Why would you think that, munchkin?" asks Creech.

"Because he said he wished he had a dog like Chance, and if he did, he'd take him home, when he was waiting on the porch."

Creech is quick on the pick-up. "On the porch?"

I jump up. I feel like I'm about to witness a crash, and I want to do anything I can to avoid it.

"You all done?" I ask Emily. "Put your plate in the dishwasher."

Happily, Em drops the subject and picks up her plate. She puts it in the rack and then turns to Creech and says, "When Mommy went in the woods. And then the policeman came."

I should have told him. I know this. I have never lied to Creech before, not in the whole lifetime I've known him. Not even when he asked if he should stay home when he had a chance of skiing on the FIS circuit with the U.S. team all those years ago. "We could be a couple," he had said then.

"A couple of what?" I'd asked, meaning it to be a joke. I knew what he meant. He meant get married. It's what everyone had expected us to do, we'd been together for so long.

He hadn't laughed.

I told him right off then I loved him.

"And I love you," he said.

We had been a couple then, but even in my

inexperience, I knew we were just two kids trying things out. We were too young for anything more serious. Both of us had things we needed to do. Creech had this burning desire for racing and the ability to do it. He needed to do it. I would always love him, but I would not hold him back. I told him as much.

He seemed relieved I felt that way. "So I should go?" he asked. I told him that of course he should. Skiing on the circuit was his dream. Of course, he should follow it.

"You want that ice cream sandwich now?" I ask Emily.

"Yes. Yes. Yes." She's jumping around, a tiny kid again.

I get out the box and offer one to Creech too. "You finish that and it's bath time," I tell Em.

"With bubbly bubbles?"

It's been a long day for both of us. Creech is eying the ice cream sandwich like it's too complex to eat. I'm ignoring him and he knows it.

"I should go," he says.

"Stay. I want to talk to you."

He wanders into the bathroom while Emily's in the tub. She's giving herself a bubble beard, white foam floating up all around her. "Ho ho ho!" she says making her voice as deep as she can. Creech doesn't laugh. He crosses his arms and watches me. I really wish that yesterday hadn't happened. It never would have if Bell were here. And I'm angry at Bell again. I've come full circle.

I get Emily into her pajamas. She's so wound up she's dancing around her room. Maybe the ice cream was a bad idea.

"School tomorrow," I tell her "We've got to get up early."

We do the monster thing. Emily bounces on the bed. I finally settle her in and after three stories, or actually the same story three times, she's ready to sleep.

I figure that Creech has given up by now, though I haven't heard the truck leave, and when I come out of Emily's room I find him sitting on the couch paging through a magazine as though he were in a doctor's waiting room. He puts the magazine down when he sees me.

"Sorry. She was a little wound up."

"I'm fairly patient, Mallory."

I sit next to him and resist the urge to take his hand. "Adam came by here last night."

"And you didn't tell me. Why?"

"Because I figured.... I don't know. I figured you'd be upset."

"And why, exactly, would you figure that?" There's a deep line where his mouth has gone taut. He pinches the top of his nose when I don't answer him. I've seen his dad do that, when one of the boys was in trouble. "Please don't tell me that you are messing around with my brother."

I pause a minute. What do I tell him? I finally say, "It's not like that."

"Then what is it like?" his voice rises. He's pretty angry. "The way I figure it, Mallo, is that you wouldn't be feeling so goddamned guilty, if you had nothing to hide."

"Nothing happened." I say quietly.

Creech gets up off the couch. "I never thought I'd ever say this to you, Mallo. But I don't fucking believe you."

Chapter Sixteen

After Creech leaves, I walk around the house. I want to pick up the phone and call him, but I don't think it would do any good. I want to talk to Bell, but I can't do that either. I need to talk to someone, so I dial my dad. It's ten o'clock, and he's surprised to hear from me. Unlike my mom, he doesn't assume the worst in my calling this late.

I tell him I just wanted to touch base and try hard to make myself sound upbeat. I talk on and on about the dog and Emily and my job, until I'm pretty sure his ear is sore. Then I stop and there's this weird silence on the line.

"So why are you really calling, sweetie?" he asks.

And I'm ready to cry again, except that I'm too old to go crying to Daddy. He wouldn't know what to do with it, if I did.

"I thought me and Em might come visit once the season's done." The thought has just popped into my head, as likely an excuse as any.

"That would be great." He sounds like he really means it. "About the middle of April, maybe? Bell ought to be home by then."

The mention of Bell is enough to do me in and I find I'm telling him all my troubles, about Roddie and Bell's continuing despite what happened. About how scared I feel. "And Creech is pissed at me, too," I finish, though I don't even try to explain this part.

"Creechie will come around. He always does."

But I don't know. He didn't seem very willing to come around when he left here.

I don't feel much better after I hang up. What I'd really like to do is pack up and take Emily down to Wells right now. If this was seven years ago and there was no Emily and no Bell, I might go running home. But it's not seven years ago, and it's not so easy to just pick up and go. I have my job to consider. I couldn't leave Albie in a lurch. It wouldn't be right.

I go to bed but I don't sleep. I tell myself I'd better stop obsessing. I'm going to pay for my insomnia tomorrow, but it doesn't seem to matter what I tell myself. I keep playing my conversation with Creech over in my head. How could I have made him see it differently?

Then I get mad, thinking it's really none of Creech's business in the first place. He has no right to be upset with me. But that doesn't sit well either.

Then I switch channels and think about Danny and try to imagine Bell running to his grandfather because I wouldn't marry him. And now I've nearly cheated on him. How could I betray his trust like that?

There's still some kind of promise between us. Even if it's unwritten.

Isn't there?

After Bell's accident, the last time he attempted West Rib, I slept the whole of two weeks in Anchorage in Bell's hospital room, sometimes in the chair near his bed, sometimes in the other bed that remained unoccupied during his stay. I was too scared to leave. The doctors said he would be fine, but I had a hard time believing it. I had this crazy thought if I left, he wouldn't be fine at all. Bell was lucky and young and very strong. Looking at him today, or even later that year, you'd never guess what he'd lived through.

He was still pretty messed up when we came home. It was summer by then. Bell couldn't get up the stairs at first and had to sleep on a rollaway bed we set up in the great room. By September he was hobbling around on crutches. By October he was nearly healed, though he still walked with a limp.

The accident had changed him. He didn't talk about the fall at first—wouldn't or couldn't—but you could see how it had affected him and not just physically, like there was more gravity around him.

In November, he went back to building the chairs for our table. He stood in the great room with a lathe in his hand, soothing the wood to smoothness. He was intent on the work, cutting, measuring, fitting. The floor around him was littered with long curls of wood that smelled pungent, a new wood smell I will always associate with Bell. I sat and watched. There was a silence between us. Not a prickly silence, the kind that festers like an undressed wound, but a quietude. A fine silence, comfortable as the late afternoon sun that streamed in through the windows.

I remember Bell looked up, something of a shadow crossing over him. "I'm sorry," he said, the words so out of context I had no idea what it was he was apologizing for. He looked forlorn in that moment, and I went over and put my hands to his shoulders, the firm bones under his shirt jutted against my palms. He put his hands to mine. "I didn't want to put you all out," he said. "I mean, I've kind of left it to you to take care of things."

"It's okay," I said. And, really, it was. He hadn't been hard to care for. A little impatient, maybe. But also determined. Besides, he was back on his feet. He had recovered.

He let go my hand and went back to working on the chair. He was measuring spokes for the back, piecing them into the seat. It amazes me how careful his hands are when he builds. You would never know it, watching him ski a slide or a glade. He's all body then, all sharp turns and angles, his legs and arms all hammer and spring. Yet with this task, he takes his time, his hands grow soft, measured.

They are that way with me too. Soft. Measured. Slow.

"I've never done a dixie like that." His voice had slowed like his hands, soft as the rustle of air pulling in from the window. "It was wild. There was nothing to hang on to. I kept tumbling and I thought, 'God, so this is how it is. This is what it feels like to die.' I didn't think I'd live through it."

"But you did. You're here."

He set the spoke down on the seat of the chair and put his arms around my waist. "I guess there are limits," he said. "I never used to think so."

My ear against his chest, I could feel the steady thump of his heart, smell the sweat and wood of him. His lips were in my hair then, and on my neck and pretty soon our clothes dropped around us like wood shards and we were on the floor.

Afterwards, he held on to me and said, "I know I take a lot of chances, Mallory," as though he were making a confession.

"Calculated risks," I said.

"Yeah. But I promise you I'll calculate them

first from now on. I don't want to go through that again."

Maybe it wasn't a direct promise. He never did say he wouldn't try the West Rib again. And maybe, over time, the calculations change, his brush with death thrown further and further into the past, until he could calculate the risk in his favor.

I turn on my pillow. There's light coming in from the skylight, a muted kind of brightness, moon reflecting on white. It has started to snow.

By morning any signs of the short jaunt we'd made into spring are erased under a wide, white universe. Snow is still coming down hard, piling onto the porch rail and the roof of the Jeep. I'm going to have to plow out, if I have any hope of getting to the hill, and I might as well do it before Emily gets up.

I'm wondering, here in the middle of March, whether the snow is a blessing or a curse. Not long ago, I wouldn't have hesitated to go with blessing. Anything to extend the season and keep me on skis. Now I'm not so sure. There's a part of me that's anxious and ready for spring.

The snow blower starts after two yanks. I've christened it 'The Monster,' and it roars loudly enough to scare every small animal within a mile radius of the cabin. I worry the noise will wake Emily, and sure enough, as I take the second turn along the drive, she's at the door in her pajamas, hopping up and down and rubbing her arms. She waves to me, and I wave back, thinking I'm going to have to stop and get her back inside. But she's got more sense than I give her credit for. Soon enough, she's gone back in and shut the door behind her.

Now I start worrying about what she's getting into.

I hurry the job as much as I can and go in after her. Nothing is broken and she's not bleeding. She is, in fact, standing in the door of her bedroom fully dressed. And, except for the mismatched socks, one red and one purple, to which she says "But I like them that way, Mom," she's done an admirable job.

"Long johns?" I question, knowing they aren't her favorite apparel. She pulls the elastic at the top of pants to show me. "Wow, I'm impressed,"

She looks at me like I'm being a fool. Of course, she can take care of herself.

The road is awful. The plow must have done a pass over our road, because there was a snowbank at the end of our drive this morning, but you wouldn't know it now. I manage to blast the Jeep through. The main road isn't much better; the road surface is covered in snow, which, having taken a respite while we were packing up, has started again. I turn the wipers on full speed and blast the defroster, so it becomes downright tropical inside the cab. I'm driving as fast as I can without cutting a cookie. All I can see is the tiny patch of road in front of me and the long spikes of snow we are combing through. I'm counting off the miles. It isn't far to the hill, but right now it feels as though I'm trying to go cross country on a lawnmower.

"Mommy, I'm hot."

I turn for a moment to see Emily's face has gotten red. I reach to turn down the defroster. "Unzip your jacket."

"I think it's stucked," she says.

"Try again, sweetie."

"I can't do it, Mom."

I turn again. The zipper is caught on her

pullover. There's not much that I can do about it. I turn back to see the snowplow, a flash of orange through the snow, coming right for us.

I swerve out of its path and skid into the other lane. Emily screams. Thoughts of a head-on collision fly through my brain. The Jeep turns, out of control, jumps the snow bank and stops with a jerk. There's a tree within touching distance of the windshield.

The breath I'd been holding rushes from my body. It's deathly still in the cab and my air sounds like a tire releasing.

"Mommy?" Emily's voice sounds wonderfully normal.

"Yeah, sweetie. We're okay," I say it to convince myself. I'm not sure I'm convinced. "Are you okay?"

"Uh-huh. My zipper's still stucked."

The Cherokee is stalled out. I pull the keys from the ignition and put the Jeep into first gear, though God knows that it's not going anywhere anyway. I can't open the door. I push against it hard and it plows the snow braced up against it into a wide arc. The falling snow slants sideways into me, and I shut the door again. My hands are shaking. I have this urge to grab Emily and just hold onto her. I glance back at her. She's looking at me expectantly, trusting I'll know what to do next. I notice the equipment bags have shifted and are wedged against the back window and that nothing has spilled.

There's a tap on the window glass and I nearly jump out of my skin. I turn to see a man bundled in an orange coat with a DPW crest and a woolen hat pulled down over his eyebrows, peering into the window. It takes me a minute to register who this is. I can't roll down the window with the engine off, so I open the door again and almost knock the poor guy over. He's standing knee deep in snow.

"I saw you skid," the words tumble from his mouth. "My God, I thought you were going to plow into that tree. My God."

I think he's as shook as I am. In the rearview mirror, I see the plow truck up against a snow bank, the orange lights circulating, the driver's door open, snow flying into the cab.

"Are you okay?" he asks.

Stupid question. Of course, we are. Of course, we're not.

"Yes," I manage. "But I think I'm wedged in pretty good."

He looks down at the tires, or where the tires would be if they weren't under a foot of snow. "I can't get you out now. But my brother, he has a tow truck. We could give you a tow once the snow stops." He looks up at the sky. "Weather service says around noon."

We can't stay here until noon I tell him. He looks at me like I'm not too bright. His eyes are hooded. He looks like he's been up all night. He probably has.. "I'll give you and the little girl a lift. Not a lot of room in the cab, but it's warm."

I try to think how far I am from Whiteface. I don't want to go to work. I don't want to drop Emily off with Charlotte. I want to take Emily and climb back into bed, pull the covers over both our heads. I want Bell there with us. I want someone to give us cocoa and tell us it will be okay.

"I have a friend who doesn't live far from here," I hear myself say. And before I know what's next, Emily and I are in the cab of the plow truck with our gear bags heading towards Creech's place.

Creech is taking the day off to drive Adam to

the airport. I had all but forgotten about what happened with Adam and about Creech being pissed at me. It's too late to think about it now. The plow driver, whose name is Artie, is turning up Creech's road. It's only a quarter mile to Creech's driveway from here.

Chapter Seventeen

Artie talks at me incessantly. I'm grateful for the warm cab, and the fact he cared enough to stop, but I'm not really listening. I hug Emily, maybe a little too tightly, though she doesn't say boo about it. Artie tells me he's been up since one and he's tired but happy for the overtime. He tells me about his brother who owns a garage over in Wilmington Notch and tows for Triple A. "But don't you worry," he says. "It ain't going to cost you."

I tell him I have Triple A and I'll be happy to pay whatever. I tell him thank you for the fourteenth time.

When we pull up Creech's drive, I almost hope the truck is gone and I'll have to ask Artie to drop me at home. But there the vehicle stands, mired in the yet-unplowed driveway. Artie gives me his brother's card after writing his home number and the DPW number on the back. He promises to bring the Jeep here "if she's running" and I thank him for the fifteenth time.

Creech is at the window, watching the plow. Wondering, no doubt, why it's stopped in front of his driveway. When I get out with Em and our stuff, he leaves the window and is at the door before I can reach it. I stop on the top step of the porch. I've got Emily by one hand and both bags hanging from the other. I must look like a refuge from some war-torn country, because Creech comes out of the house in his bare feet and takes the bags from me before hopping back in through the front door. We follow him in and Emily and I stand in his front room dripping onto the linoleum.

I kneel down to undo Emily's zipper. It's not too deeply embedded into the wool of her sweater and unzips easily.

Emily looks up at Creech. "Mommy crashed the car," she says, matter-of-fact as an anchorwoman on the six o'clock news.

Words suddenly find their way from my brain to my mouth and I unload on Creech about the plow and the Cherokee and the snow bank and the tree and Artie and Artie's brother.

Creech stops me before I get to Artie's brother's garage. "Slow down," he says. And I stop talking altogether.

Emily takes off her coat. She holds it so it drags against the floor, which is where she has deposited her hat and mittens. Creech takes it from her, scoops up the hat and mittens, and I realize that I'm still in my coat and hat and gloves. It's pretty warm inside. I hand him my stuff, too.

He points towards the kitchen "Help yourself to coffee. I just made a pot."

He comes in while I'm standing at the coffee pot with an empty ceramic mug in my hand and staring at the orange Formica counter that tops Creech's ancient dark pine cabinets. He takes the cup from me and pours coffee into it, pours a dollop of milk in after the coffee, and hands the mug back. "Drink this," he says. Then he asks Em if she wants cocoa, and he zaps a cup of water in the microwave and shakes the contents of a packet of Swiss Miss into the bubbling liquid.

I find my way to the kitchen table and sit down. Emily comes over and crawls into my lap.

"I should call Albie," I say, remembering I

should have been at work by now.

Creech hands me his phone. Albie's at the station and I tell him what happened. I'm surprised I can be so calm in the telling. He tells me to take care of myself and Emily and not to worry about coming in. It's quiet up on the hill. A strange irony of ski areas is that snowstorms tend to slow things down because no one can get there.

"Better?" asks Creech after I hand back the phone. Emily has climbed off my lap and found her own chair. She's sipping at the cocoa Creech has set in front of her.

"Yeah, thanks."

The stairs creak and Adam calls down his flight's been cancelled. He stops dead at the kitchen door. I know I'm probably the last person he wanted to see today. I look at my cup. There's a hairline fracture running the length of the blue ceramic. I am studying this when Adam whirls past.

"Hello, Mallory." My name runs like an annoyed sigh from his mouth.

"Hello," I say back, and he turns to Creech. "I'm going to finish packing" He grabs his coffee and retreats.

I watch him walk out and wonder how I ever could have been dumb enough to get myself involved with him in the first place.

Creech is looking out the window. The snow's still coming down at a steady clip. "I should shovel out the drive," he says. "Your skis still on the Jeep?"

"Yeah, I couldn't bring them along."

"I'll go get them."

I don't want him or anyone else out on that road. "It's okay. It can wait."

Once we're done with this exchange, there's an

awkward silence neither of us seems to be able to get past.

Emily breaks it for us. "Mommy, are we going to stay here a long time?"

"For a while, if it's okay with Creech." I look at him. "Artie says he can bring the Jeep here around noon. Is that okay?" I sound tentative. Since he's not about to kick us out, I'm not giving him much of a choice.

"It's fine, Mallory." He doesn't sound like it's fine at all. "Why wouldn't it be?"

"Can I go watch TV?" asks Em. Our TV at the cabin has no antennae, and we don't get cable. Which means on a good day, we get one channel with shadows and snow. As a consequence of this, Emily thinks TV is a huge treat. I can't imagine there'd be much on to hold her interest at this hour.

"Sure, knock yourself out, munchkin," says Creech.

I follow Em to the front room where Creech's TV is perched on a small table between two windows. Creech has a satellite, though why he thinks he needs this is beyond me. He says it's for ESPN, and I would guess this is about the only station he watches. Sure enough, Sports Center jumps into focus when I turn on the set. I flip around until I find Blue's Clues.

"I know this one," says Em, taking a seat on Creech's secondhand couch. "It's Blue the dog."

I leave Emily to the dog and wander back to the kitchen where Creech is buttering a slice of toast.

"You want something to eat?" he asks.

"No thanks."

He wraps the toast in a paper towel and makes

for the door.

"Creech, wait," I say. I can't stand the unsaid between us anymore. It's a huge gap, like the crevasse Roddie fell into. "We should talk."

"There's nothing to talk about."

I pull out the chair next to mine with my foot. "Yeah, there is."

He comes over, plops into the chair, and sets his toast on the table. "What is it with women," he says to no one in particular and certainly not to me, "that they have to talk about everything?"

I ignore the comment. "I hate that you're pissed at me."

"I'm not pissed."

What is it about men, I want to say but don't, that they can't own up to things? I give him a look. He gets up, pours himself another cup of coffee, and refills my cup. "Since it looks like you plan on keeping me here," he says.

He's examining the pie-shaped table. I know he's thinking out what to say. Or not to say.

"I should have told you right off. About Adam," I say, helping him out.

"You can do what you want, Mallory. You don't need my permission."

"Nothing happened, Creech. You've got to believe me. Ask Adam."

Creech turns his coffee mug. It says 'Whiteface Mountain' on the front of it. He studies this as though he's never read it before. "I did ask Adam. He told me it was none of my business. He also said a few other things I'd rather not repeat." He looks at me again. "I believe you, Mallory. Okay?" He takes a gulp of coffee. "So, are we square?"

"I hope so." I put my hand on top of his and he doesn't pull back. "Thanks for putting up with me."

154

"Shit, Mallo. Somebody's got to." He smiles at me and stands. "You can help me shovel," he says. "Payment for food and shelter."

I check on Emily, who is heavy into Blue's Clues. She barely nods when I tell her that I'll be right outside. The snow has stopped. Creech hands me a shovel. He hasn't bought a snow blower yet, and so we have to clear the snow the old fashioned way. It's a heavy snow and there's a good foot of it. Clearing it is sweaty work, and I like that it keeps my mind off other things like Bell being gone and my Jeep in a ditch. Pretty soon Creech and I are laughing like a couple of kids. We dump snow on one another with the shovels and race to see who can shovel fastest. I glance up and see Adam in the upstairs window watching us.

When we come in we are both drenched from the inside out. I feel better than I have in weeks, and in this spirit I offer to make us a big breakfast.

"Think I can survive your cooking?" Creech asks.

I smack him on the back with a dishtowel just as Adam comes into the kitchen.

"You two are cozy," he says. There's an edge to his voice. I stop myself from saying something nasty. Creech has stopped smiling. Adam shakes his head. "Scruples, my ass," he mutters under his breath and he turns to go out the door.

This is too much. I block his way. "What is that supposed to mean?"

"You know damn well what it means."

"No, really. Maybe you can explain it to me."

Creech looks like he's suddenly found himself in a cage full of hungry tigers.

"Guys," he says. "You both need to chill."

"You weren't so chilled last night, big brother,

155

when you thought I was fucking darling little Mallo."

Creech doesn't get mad often, but when he does it is not a pretty sight. He grabs Adam by the collar and shoves him up against the wall. "You've got a smart mouth, you know?" he says. His teeth are clenched. If it weren't so real, it might be funny.

Before anything more can happen, Creech, luckily, seems to come to his senses. He lets go of Adam and looks at his hands as though he can't believe what he just did. Adam doesn't say anything more. He gives Creech a nasty look, then shoots the same look at me and leaves the room.

"How about that breakfast or brunch or whatever the hell you were just promising," Creech says. "Then I'll go down and get your skis."

There's this live wire, all disconnected, running between us. The electricity's leaping off the walls. I don't know what to do about it, so I do the only thing I can do—hunt through the cupboards for a pan, check the fridge for eggs, go out to Emily who is watching Sesame Street.

"Do you want breakfast, sweetie?

She nods and asks what Adam's doing, pointing to the window behind the set. I look out to see him sitting in the snow bank beyond the sagging porch. He's not wearing a jacket, and I can see one bare foot where it sticks out into the newly shoveled drive. He used to pull this kind of thing all the time when we were kids. Only then he'd sit in the snow in his underwear when he was mad. "Cools him off," his brothers would say. Sitting out there, he seems like a little kid and I find that I'm feeling just a little sorry for him.

I make scrambled eggs, using up the whole dozen stashed in the fridge. Creech makes a new

156

pot of coffee and pops slices of bread into the toaster two at a time. When we're done, I call Emily and we sit down together.

"Adam's still in the snow," she says, as though this worries her and maybe we ought to fix it.

Creech looks at me. I think he's thinking the same thing I am—if his brother's nuts enough to freeze his balls then let him sit. Then he looks at Em. "I guess I'll go tell him I'm sorry," he says, not looking the least bit apologetic. I imagine them getting into it again, can picture them wrestling in the snow.

"I'll go," I say, though I don't want to. Last thing I want is to get into the middle of all this. But I'm already in the middle anyway, and my little girl is reminding me that going out there is the mature thing to do. I make up a plate of eggs and toast and walk outside. It's warmed some, and being out without a coat isn't as tough as I'd thought it would be.

"Peace offering," I say to Adam, handing him the plate.

He grabs it and mumbles something under his breath that makes me want to ask him how old he thinks he is. And that maybe he ought to act his age.

"Your mother would make you come inside," I say.

"Good thing she's not here then, isn't it?"

"Look, for what it's worth, I'm sorry. I never should have let things get as far as they did. I don't want to come in between you and Creech."

"Yeah, well," he says and takes a bite of toast.

"You're not going to accept my apology and forgive me?"

"For what? Making me feel like shit? Or driving

Creech nuts? Or both?"

"I don't drive Creech nuts." I say. I'm about ready to push him into the snow bank and go inside. Let him freeze his ass.

When he looks at me, it's like he's just discovered something that he doesn't quite believe. "You don't get it, do you?"

"Get what? There's nothing to get except that you are certifiable."

"God, Mallory. My brother is crazy about you. He always has been. Poor dumb fuck."

"That's stupid. We're friends. We've been friends for a long time."

"Yup. You two were pretty friendly in high school. Making out in Creech's room."

"High school was a long time ago. None of us are in high school anymore."

"I know. I heard the speech. Responsibility. Relationship. No free agency. I hear it from both of you. Creech tells me how much you love Bell. Bell does what he wants, and I can guarantee you, responsibility isn't in the man's vocabulary. But what the hell? You love him."

He's hit a nerve and I feel the tears rise up. "It's a two-way street. Bell loves me. He loves Emily." I'm saying it to convince myself as much as to convince him.

"That's what you keep telling yourself, isn't it? But anyone with eyes can see that you're not convinced."

The tears are streaming down my cheeks now. How dare he say those things to me? How dare he be right?

"That's the truth, isn't it, Mallory? And you don't know where you stand. Otherwise, we wouldn't be having this little conversation."

158

"You want the truth? Truth is—you're right. Truth is—he might not be back. Bell could end up like Roddie, and Emily will grow up without a daddy." I swipe at the tears rolling down my face. "I don't know if I can even live with him anymore. Maybe it would be better to call it quits and take Emily and move back to Wells." I shout this last bit at him.

Adam looks horrified that I'd lose my cool like this. But he's not looking at me; he's looking behind me to the door.

I turn to see Creech and my little girl in the doorway. My little girl, turning and running for cover.

Chapter Eighteen

"Shit," I say under my breath, wanting to sock both brothers for bringing this on. Mostly, though, I'm mad at myself for pulling the plug and letting it fly.

"Christ. I'm sorry, Mallory," says Adam

I pay him no mind. I don't care what he thinks or doesn't think.

Emily is curled into a ball on Creech's couch. The count on Sesame Street is counting bats. I turn him off at seven. "Em..." I sit down by her head, she pulls herself tighter. I touch her hair and she pulls away.

Creech comes in with his hands jammed into his pockets. "The tow guy's here," he says. I try touching Emily again, but she won't let me. Better to let her stew awhile. She'll get past it. Maybe.

Artie's at the front door, my skis propped against his shoulder. He hands me Emily's skis, as though he needs to give me something for showing up here. "My brother Al, he towed your vehicle up to the garage in Wilmington. It's still running and all, but it needs a major front-end alignment." He balances my skis against the door jamb. "Thought you might want these." Behind him is not the snowplow, but a beat-up Crown Victoria, still running in the driveway. Artie goes to the backseat and takes out Emily's booster. "You'll need this, too," he says.

I thank him again for being so kind and Creech offers him coffee, but he can probably sense it's a terrible time for hospitality. He says he wouldn't want to trouble and off he goes back to his car. I yell thanks again, agitated by the thought that I've treated him with less grace than I would have liked, considering all he's done.

Adam's not in the snow bank anymore. He's not anywhere. "Maybe we should go," Creech says. He takes my skis and Em's and puts them in the bed of his truck. I go back into the front room, where Emily's still curled in a ball. I sit by her head again.

"Time to go home," I say, not wanting to reach out and have her recoil again.

"No." Her voice is muffled by the couch cushion.

"We have to go home now, Emily." This is the wrong tactic, no matter how gently I say it. I should tell her I'm sorry. That sometimes mommies say things they don't really mean. Trouble is she'd know I was lying to her.

She uncurls and looks at me, her eyes shot through with tears and anger, her nose running enough that I'd wipe it if I thought it wouldn't start a tantrum. "I don't want to go with you," she screeches, her four-year-old voice near hysteria. "You made Chance go away. And you made Daddy go away." She starts sobbing again, big huffy snuffling tears. I reach out for her shoulder and she scoots away and runs for the front door.

I'm after her almost as soon as she's up. Though she's quick, she's only four and no match for an adult. I catch her on the front porch. The tantrum I'd hoped to avoid has blossomed full and ugly. She kicks and screams. I hold on to her, hoping I'm not hurting her.

"Let go!" she sobs. "Let go!"

I wrestle her into the back of Creech's cab, telling her over and over, as calmly as I can, that she needs to stop it. Creech has the wherewithal to gather up our coats and bags, which he stows next to Em.

She's still squirming around, but she's calmed some. Big angry tears spill from her eyes. "I hate you! I hate you! I hate you!"

It takes all I've got to ignore her. I climb into the front of the cab, as shaky as I was after the accident.

When we pull into our driveway and I let her out of the seat, Emily stalks off into the house without a word or a look in our direction. Creech unloads my stuff. "Want me to stick around?"

I do, really. But I can't do that—to him or to me. It's my problem and I have to solve it.

"I'll be okay."

"You sure?"

"Yeah. She'll calm down. It'll be fine." I try to sound confident, but I'm not and I'm pretty sure he can read this.

I find Emily in her room, sitting cross-legged in her closet with her thumb stuffed into her mouth. She hasn't sucked her thumb in over a year. I sit down next to the door and she crawls deeper into the space, disrupting shoes and boots. She takes the thumb out and tells me to go away.

"I don't want to go away. I want to talk with you, Em." I don't get any response. "Your Daddy loves you, baby. He'll come back." The words stick in my throat, all my fear lurching forward.

"That's not what you said. You said he's never coming back. Never never." Her hurt words are

162

thorns, spit from her mouth.

"I was just mad, Emily. I said it because I was mad."

"I want to call Daddy. I want to talk to him right now."

I start to say we can't, get ready to give her all the same old reasons why we can't. But then I think maybe we ought to try. Maybe I can patch through. I'm willing to try for Emily, willing to cut through three thousand miles and mountains.

"We can try. I can't promise we'll get through."

Emily climbs out of the closet, walks to the living room, and hands me the phone. She sticks her thumb back into her mouth and waits. I get as far as the Talkeetna ranger station.

"Sorry, ma'am. It's stormy up on Denali. We haven't been able to patch anything through for nearly twenty-four hours. Is it an emergency?"

I want to say yes, my daughter's heart is breaking, but in truth, we are here, Emily and I, whole bodied and breathing and there is no cause for alarm. I tell him no. I thank him and I hang up reluctant to face my daughter.

"The weather's bad, sweetie. Daddy's up too high to talk to. We can check the Daddy Site, if you want."

Emily pops out her thumb, fresh tears popping into her eyes. "No. I want to talk to Daddy." Her voice is fierce, I feel helpless against it.

"We can't." I wish that the phone would ring. That Bell would be on the other end of the line.

"I want to talk."

"Emily."

She glares at me and stomps off to the porch. She sits in the snow, having learned Adam's trick of cooling off. It's warm enough, the afternoon sun lapping the eaves of the cabin leaving islands of almost spring. I decide to let her be. For a little while, I'll just let her be.

I go upstairs and check the website. The wintry weather the ranger mentioned so casually has me worried. Bell ought to be making the descent now, ought to be on his way back. Not knowing exactly where he is only exacerbates the worry. My mind trails along the stories I've heard, flipping channels on catastrophe: Trapped on a ledge, two climbers survive thirty-mile-an-hour winds; a climber dies of exposure in a freak snowstorm; a climber steps into a crevasse and suffers massive trauma despite the rope. There is nothing I can do, three thousand miles from Bell, except worry. If I could stop thinking it would be better.

I find the site. The old file photo, with Roddie and Bell both smiling, is still posted. He's happy anyway. He loves that mountain like a drug. I want to chase this last thought more than the others. The last update came in a few days ago. "Nearing the summit. Will attempt the ski tomorrow, if the weather holds."

That was a few days ago. Now the storm's moved in and Bell and the rest of the team are somewhere above eighteen thousand feet. Possibly, they are stranded. I wish I could patch through. Like Emily, I think I didn't try hard enough. And then here's a new thought—the whole trouble with Bell and me lies in lack of trying.

I hear a rustling downstairs and think Emily has finally come inside. I rush down, but she's not at the door. And when I look, she's not on the porch either.

I call out to her and she doesn't answer me. I

look in her room, check the closet and under the bed. I look in the bathroom, pulling back the curtain for the tub.

"Emily, this isn't funny. Come out right now."

No response. I'm seeking, but she doesn't want to be found. I put on my jacket and go outside. I look under the porch, in the garage, under the slide of the swing set. I tell myself not to panic. She's a good hider; she'll come out eventually. The panic's there anyway. It's a physical sensation that rides up from my feet, through my spine, and threatens to close my throat.

I'm not sure why I do it, but something compels me to look up. And there, in the top branches of the maple, some twenty feet off the ground, sits my daughter. The panic seizes my heart and squeezes it. She's climbed the tree before, but she's never gone up so high.

I find my voice and try to make it calm. "Emily, you need to get down from there."

"No," she says and she crawls farther out onto the branch.

"Emily, please come down."

"I don't want to."

"Emily. Right now." I'm sure she can hear my panic. It's swirling around the yard like a tornado.

She gets her feet out under her and begins to stand up on the limb.

"Emily, no!" I scream this, I'm sure of it.

She looks down and her foot slips. I see it slide slow motion. It skates from the limb. Her hands reach out to grab hold of the wood, and they slip too.

There's a thwack of branches, a conspiratorial snapping of twigs. And in one heartbeat's time, my little girl is sprawled at the base of the tree, as limp

and still as the afternoon air.

Chapter Nineteen

The world has gone silent. Nothing moves. The ground under Emily is soft with new fallen snow, and I'm thankful for this small mercy. I squat down next to her and put my ear to her sweater. Emily's breath comes up warm against my cheek. I can hear the steady thump of her heart. She doesn't open her eyes when I call her name. I check her limbs. There are no obvious contusions. I pull her eyelids back to check her pupils. They are both the same size. There is no fluid running from her ears, and she is not bleeding. All good signs. But she doesn't open her eyes when I call her name.

I take off my jacket and drape it around her. Her arm is swollen, and I think it may be broken. I've left my phone on the dining room table and I need to get it so I can call 911. I don't want to leave her here limp and alone.

"I'll be right back, honey," I tell her, though she can't answer me.

I run inside, grab the phone, and punch numbers as I run back out. I get 911 Dispatch. Robin Hatcher. The name jumps into my head. I tell Robin what's wrong. I'm sure she can hear my panic. My voice is shaking, I have to gulp to speak at all. I tell her where I am and she says an ambulance will be right there. I tell her to hurry, as though they might not.

I feel a shiver go up my arms when a breeze kicks in. I'm kneeling in the snow without my jacket. I realize this might not be wise. It doesn't matter. If anything happens to Emily, nothing else will matter. I check her pulse again. It's steady. Her breathing is regular.

This is a good sign. A very good sign. But she's been out for a while. More than five minutes. Grade five concussion, the words from EMT training rush in at me. That means one of two things. Option A, she'll wake up as though nothing ever happened. She may have to slow down a bit, but she'll be fine. Option B reminds me of the day we brought Johnny Ahern down on the sled after he dixied head first into a tree in the glades. He never saw his seventeenth birthday. Grade 5 concussion. That's how it began.

I tell myself to stop. I can't think like this. It would be better if I couldn't think at all. If I could just lie down next to Emily and stop thinking.

I hear a murmur. I say Emily's name again, but there's no response. It's just the wind flying through the hemlocks avalanching the snow from the branches. Time passes with alarming slowness, if it passes at all. Finally, I hear the soft report of a siren in the distance. It's the most beautiful sound I've ever heard.

The sound deepens, the volume of it increases. I think about our near miss this morning. How grateful I was not hitting that tree. Fate wanted us, me and Emily. It wanted us badly enough to come try again. It had better aim this time.

I see lights threading through the trees. The siren stops. A voice calls out my name. "Mallory? Where are you?" The familiarity is a balm. Someone I know. Someone who'll help me take care of my baby.

"I'm in the back," I yell. And then I see them. Stan Dykstra, a husky little guy who was in my

EMT class. Stan, who told me once that his parents named him Stanley after the hockey trophy. And another guy who looks vaguely familiar, carrying a child-sized spine board. He looks a little like Abe Lincoln and I wonder if this is why I think I recognize him.

Stan kneels down opposite me alongside Emily. "She fell?" he asks.

I nod and point up. Both men peer into the tree. They don't show it, but I know what they are thinking. It's the same thing I'm thinking: My God, it's a long flight down from there.

"She's been out the whole time?" Stan asks.

"Yes. Her pulse and respiration are normal though." I want him to tell me that this is a good sign. I know that it's a good sign. But he doesn't say anything at all. He just nods towards the other guy.

"This is Chuck Anders," he says by way of introduction.

The tall man nods. "You know my sister, Kristen." Maybe that's why he seems familiar.

I stand back and watch them work. They strap Emily to the board. Chuck goes back to the ambulance for a stretcher. Stan puts a neck brace on her and checks her ears again for fluid. Although I've already done this three or four times, I don't say anything. He wraps a space blanket around her, tosses me my jacket, and tells me to put it on.

"You can ride up front with Chuck," says Stan as they load Emily onto the ambulance. She looks awful; the backboard like a papoose, a strap running over her forehead, a neck brace holding her tight.

"No," I say. "I'm riding in the back with you."

Stan and Chuck exchange a look. "I can't let you do that, Mallory," says Stan.

"Yes, you can. I'm certified. I've ridden in the back before." I jump in after the stretcher. If they want me to ride in the front, one of them is going to have to extract me physically.

I sit next to Emily's head and stroke her cheek, hoping for a response. I get nothing, though her vitals remain good.

Her vitals are good, I tell myself all through the ride. I repeat it like a mantra under the siren's scream.

The hospital is a shriek of bright lights. Over and over I'm asked what happened. Over and over I tell the story. In each telling I hear my lack of vigilance, my neglect, my absence. I try to excuse it, but I can't. Emily climbed that tree while I was busy worrying over Bell.

This is the bottom line. My worry over Bell caused my little girl's fall. If I hadn't gone upstairs to check the website—or, better, if Bell had never gone back to Denali in the first place—my little girl would be home eating dinner right now instead of lying in an emergency room with an IV stuck in her arm.

The ER doctor is Rick Ferris. I've worked with him any number of times in conjunction with Whiteface rescues and emergencies. He's a middle-aged guy, even-tempered, steady and competent. Just the kind of doctor you'd want in your corner during an emergency. It's a real comfort to me that he's on Emily's case, though when he suggests I go and get some coffee while he examines her, I say no. After his exam, Dr. Ferris orders X-rays.

He eyes me cautiously. "She could wake up anytime," he says. "I've seen it happen."

"How often?" Visions of Johnny Ahern are dancing through my brain.

"Sometimes," he says. "If she wakes up in the next twenty-four hours, her chances are good."

"And after that?"

"They go down considerably."

They wheel Emily down to radiology. The stretcher squeaks over the polished tile floors. I wait in the hall. There is a line of plastic chairs that look tortuous to sit in. I pace instead. I count tile squares. There are ten black squares to the door at the end of the hall. I promise whatever power that be if Emily comes through all this okay, I'll be the best, most attentive mother who ever graced the planet Earth.

"It's bad, isn't it?" I say when Dr. Ferris comes back with the X-rays. He's tacked the picture of Emily's cranium to the light. Her head looks tiny and foreign in the negative of bones.

"The skull's not fractured," he says. "That's good news." He tacks up a picture of her arm, and another of her spine. "Spine looks good too. Which is really good news. There is a hairline fracture in her radius." He points to a spidery thread woven into the tapestry of Emily's arm bone. "Not too serious. We'll splint it and have it cast in a few days when the swelling goes down."

I see from the way he's looking at me that there's more. I cross my arms and brace myself for the collision I'm sure will come.

"There's some response to stimuli, which is an excellent, a really excellent sign. But..." And here it comes, the train crash. He puts his hand to my arm. "She is still in a coma. I feel very strongly that

171

she needs to be in a pediatric ICU. I'd like her taken to Burlington."

And there it is, the big ugly blinding thing I've been waiting for. I think I slump against his arm, because Dr. Ferris begins rubbing his thumb into my shoulder.

"It's precautionary, Mallory. I'd rather err on the side of caution. There's probably contusion. There's danger of subarachnoid hemorrhage. If that happens, they'll be prepared for it. They can have her in the OR in minutes."

I'm trying to sort through the words: subarachnoid, contusion, hemorrhage, OR. Euphemisms. He's telling me he's scared, too. Scared of what might happen to my little girl.

"Burlington?" I repeat stupidly.

"Yes. Fletcher Allen. They have a terrific neurology department. We'll take her by ambulance. You can ride along."

I nod. The walls of the exam room are closing in on me. Burlington. *Oh my God.*

"We've made the call already. We want to get her down there as soon as possible."

I have the sudden urge to throw up. But nothing comes. I swallow hard. "Okay. We do what we have to do." He squeezes my shoulder and walks away.

There's another firestorm of activity after that. I stand back and watch the hospital staff prepare Emily for transport. I say a few prayers, none of them kind. Angry with God, I tell the bastard to give her back to me. She's just a little girl. Go pick on someone else. I'm angry at Bell too. Greedy for his own thrills, he remains out of contact. Fine time to be out of contact. Let him stay out of contact. Let him stay in fucking Alaska forever.

The ride to Fletcher Allen is much like the ride we took earlier. Only this time, it's much longer and I don't know either of the attendants. This time, we're headed for a place miles from home where strangers will take care of my little girl.

In ICU, Emily is put into a crib in a small room with a wall-sized window that looks out into the ward. There's another flurry of activity. Another round of questions about how and where and when. Finally, everyone leaves and Em and I are left in semi-darkness. The room is silent except for the monitors that record Emily's heartbeat, pulse, and respiration.

A nurse walks in and hands me a surgical release form. "It's a precaution," he says.

The form is full of warnings and hazards. It contains the words 'possible death.' I sign it and hand it back, feeling like I'm handing over Emily's life.

The attending pediatric neurologist, Dr. Patel, is a small brown man with a soft handshake. He examines Emily, a deep furrow creasing the space between his dark eyes. "There are no external signs of trauma," he says. His voice has the singsong lilt of India mixed with Britain. "But we need to do an MRI to be sure. Hematomas can be very tricky."

Like trees, I think. Like falls. Maybe like me and Bell. Tricky. You just never know.

He looks at the chart. "She could wake up at any time," he says, "right as rain." He rolls his r's. "I've seen it happen." What he doesn't say is that sometimes it doesn't happen. Sometimes it never happens. He shakes my hand again.

They take the entire bed with Emily in it down to radiology. The nurse, who introduced herself as Melissa, says I should stay in the ICU. "They'll be back in half an hour," she says. I want to protest, but I don't. I'm feeling way, way too tired.

"Have you eaten?" Melissa asks.

The answer is no. Not since breakfast at Creech's, which seems like a lifetime ago. I'm not hungry.

"I don't think I could eat," I tell her.

"Why don't I hunt up a sandwich for you anyway? The kitchen will be closed soon, so this way you'll have it, if you change your mind."

She comes back twenty minutes later with a dinner tray—turkey on white bread, a cup of soup, a pint of milk, an ice cream cup and a cookie. She puts the tray on the stand next to the space where Emily's bed should be. I thank her. I take one bite of the sandwich. It's dry and unappealing. I put it back down and stare at it.

Ten minutes later, they wheel Emily back in. They say nothing about what they did—or did not— find. I sit next to Em's crib. There are no windows except the big one looking in toward the ward. There is no clock in the room. I hold Emily's hand and fall into a kind of stupor.

Dr. Patel comes back to say that the MRI was inconclusive. "There is no apparent hematoma," he says. "But we must keep monitoring. Sometimes they crop up after the fact. We will do another MRI in the morning."

The words 'cautious optimism' sweep through my brain. I shake Dr. Patel's hand again, and he leaves me to my brooding.

I drift off for a few minutes. Melissa comes in to tell me my husband is here. I figure I'm either dreaming or hallucinating. In the dream, Bell has heard our distress all the way on Denali. He's teleported himself here. I nod at her, and the next thing I know, Creech has his arms around me, and I'm breathing in the itchy wool of his sweater.

He kisses my forehead. "Hell of a day, huh?"

"What are you doing here?" The question is probably rude. He doesn't take offense.

"I dropped your car off at your house. No one was home and the door was wide open. Looked a little dicey, so I called around."

I give him another hug. "Thanks, baby," I say.

He shrugs this off. "How is she?" he asks taking Emily's hand.

I feel tears swell up. "They're not saying much. But the fact is we're here. And that's not good."

Chapter Twenty

"So, what did you do?" I ask Creech. "Tell them that you were PD Bell?"

"Something like that." He smiles for the first time since he got here.

"No harm in it, since the real Mr. Bell won't be making an appearance any time soon."

I feel anger rise up in my throat. I'm angry over the whole awful day. The stupid phone call the rangers couldn't patch through. Emily saying, "I want to talk to Daddy right now."

"Have you called him?" asks Creech. I shake my head. "Don't you think he ought to know?"

"If he ought to know, he ought to stay in touch."

Creech doesn't ask anymore. I do have to make some phone calls though. My cell has no juice, so I ask to borrow Creech's. I have to go down to the cafeteria, where cell phones are allowed. Creech promises to keep vigil. I make him promise to run down and get me if anything at all happens.

I call Albie and explain I won't be in tomorrow or the day after. He tells me to take all the time I need, and I begin to wonder how much time that will be. I call my mother, sure she'll tell me she told me so. That nothing good could ever come of my move to Lake Placid. That I should have married Tommy.

But she doesn't say any of those things. She asks if I need anything and tells me she'll be there first thing in the morning. Although I wouldn't have thought so, I really want her here. I call my dad, who's ready to pack up and drive to Burlington right away. I tell him Mom is coming and he says of course she is, and not in a nasty way. I call Danny. He doesn't say anything while I break the news to him. Then, right before I hang up, he says, "You get her well. You bring her home to us." I can't tell him it's not in my power anymore. Truly nothing, not Emily's getting well, not my future with Bell, is in my power anymore.

"You want me to find you a room near here?" Creech asks when I get back to the ICU. He looks road weary, and it dawns on me that he drove a long distance just to be with us.

I squeeze his shoulder and he asks, "What?"

"You go on. You look like you could use some sleep."

He puts his hand on mine and I think again what a good friend he is. The best I could ask for.

"I'll stay as long as you need me to," he says.

"I'll be okay. You find a room. I can call you, if anything changes."

"I could give you the same line."

"I know."

"But it wouldn't make any difference, would it?"

"No."

"Okay, then." Creech kisses my cheek and gives Em's hand a squeeze. There's a little tick, the slightest bit of movement. I think I imagined it, but I'm not sure.

"Squeeze her hand again."

There it is again. The slightest turn of Emily's head. Creech sees it too.

"Emily?" When I call her name, I get no response. But when I put my hand to her forehead, she moves a little.

Creech runs over to the nurse's station. The shift has changed. A new nurse, an older woman named Gloria, comes over.

I touch Emily's forehead and she twitches. "She moved." I say, finding it hard to contain my excitement.

The nurse smiles. "So she did."

"That's good, right? I mean that's a great sign."

Gloria squeezes my arm. "It's a very good sign. I'm going to call Dr. Patel."

The thing is, Emily doesn't wake up. She doesn't respond to my voice. I figured it would all happen quickly now. She'd be back to us. But she's not.

Dr. Patel comes in five minutes later. I didn't know he was still here. He shakes hands with Creech and checks Emily.

"Stimulus response," he says. "That's very nice."

"That means she's waking up, right?" I ask.

"It can mean that, yes."

There is caution in his voice. It makes me angry. I want him to tell me it's all going to be okay now and he's not doing that.

"It can, meaning...?"

"That sometimes it is a sign of recovery. Yes."

"But not always."

"No, Ms. Prescott. Not always. But it is a very positive sign."

I feel like I've received a gift and he's trashed it. Dr. Patel mumbles something to Creech and goes out again. I stare at my baby and will her to wake up. Just wake up. But she doesn't.

Creech sits back down.

"You really ought to go," I say. "You're

exhausted. I'll be all right."

"I'll stay awhile," he says.

He falls asleep in the chair, his legs splayed out to either side, his head tipped back. It would be funny, if we weren't here. I read somewhere that people in a coma can hear and that it helps to talk to them. I start talking to Emily. I tell her how much I love her. How much everybody loves her. I talk about the hill and Chance. I get to Bell and I tell her that her daddy wants her to get better too. I know, in my heart of hearts, Emily's fondest wish was to talk with Bell.

"We'll try calling him, honey," I tell her. "I'll try again and this time I won't quit until I get through."

It's one AM here, evening in Alaska. Creech's cell phone is sitting on the bed stand next to Emily. I grab it, run downstairs, and dial the number for the ranger station in Talkeetna. I get a recording that says the office is closed, but I can leave a message.

After the beep, I say I need to get in touch with PD Bell of Emily's Boys. I say it's an emergency and very important. I leave Creech's cell number and hang up thinking I should have sounded more panicked. Instead, I sounded listless. The adrenaline rush is over and all that's left is fatigue and a strong desire to go home.

I sit opposite Creech and put my hand through the bars of Emily's crib so I can cradle it against Emily's head. She feels slightly feverish, her hair sticking to my fingers as I brush my hand through it.

She turns a little. I remind myself this is a good sign. It's very hopeful. But I'm not feeling hopeful. I'm feeling defeated.

"I can't get through to Daddy right now," I tell Em. "I'll keep trying. I promise. I'll keep trying."

The quiet in the room runs over me. I drift in and out of sleep until I finally fall under. The next thing I know, a nurse brushes my chair as she bends to tend to Emily. It's a new nurse, one I don't recognize. The nurse's nametag says Karen. She tells me they are almost ready to take Emily down for another MRI.

"What time is it?" I ask her.

"About six o'clock."

Creech's chair is empty and I don't see him anywhere. I tell Emily I'll be waiting right here for her when she gets back.

Creech comes back as they wheel Emily out of the room. He's carrying two coffees and a coffee cake wrapped in cellophane. He hands me the cake. "Best the vending machine had to offer."

I take a bite. It's stale to the point of being brittle and I wonder how long it's been in the machine. "Tasty. What—they didn't have Devil Dogs?"

"Not a breakfast food." Creech hands me a coffee. "Drink this. It's terrible."

"I tried to get a hold of Bell last night. Nobody was home at the ranger station. I left your cell number."

Under normal circumstances, Creech would razz me about using his phone without asking. But these aren't normal circumstances and he doesn't say a thing. We drink lukewarm coffee in silence. Creech is right. It's terrible.

Another nurse comes over, another new face. She tells me they want me down in radiology. I feel the panic rising again. Yesterday they as much as told me to stay here. Now they want me there. This can't be good. The words subarachnoid hematoma, along with frontal contusion and surgery stampede through my brain.

"Which way?" I ask the nurse and I'm off before she can say any of those things and make them real. Creech is after me.

Radiology is on the first floor, two floors below the ICU. We get lost twice on the way there. The reception area is empty when we arrive, and I don't know which way to turn. I'm about to go postal, when a woman in pink scrubs comes out of nowhere and asks if we are Emily Bell's parents.

We follow the woman back through a long corridor at the end of which is a large room with a huge white coffin-like machine. Emily is lying in front of the machine's tubular opening. Only she's not lying there. She's thrashing. Convulsion is my first thought, but then I hear her.

"No, no, no!" Over and over. The technicians gathered around Emily part to make way for me.

"Emily?" I say.

Emily stops twisting and looks at me as though I'm part of a dream she's having. Not a good dream. I put my hand to her head. If it was warm last night, it's downright steamed up now.

"Emily," I say again, and the room starts swimming away.

"Mommy?"

"Yeah, baby. You had a bad fall. We had to go to the hospital."

Emily's eyes start to focus. "Make them stop, Mommy."

I give them an evil look. I'm ready to kill them for scaring my little girl. I know they didn't do it on purpose, but that doesn't matter.

"We had her in the machine," the woman in pink says.

Another woman, a dark-haired woman in yellow scrubs says they haven't gotten the pictures yet.

Emily's eyes flit person to person. She's squeezing my hand so hard that there's no blood left in it.

"Can we go back upstairs?" I ask.

"We need to wait for the doctor," says the woman in yellow. "He's been called."

"How long until he gets here?" I ask.

"We don't know." The woman in yellow takes a step towards Emily, her grip on my hand tightens enough to make my fingers throb.

"I want my little girl taken back upstairs." I say. "We can wait for the doctor there."

"It would be much more efficient to wait here," says the woman in yellow.

The woman in pink hasn't said anything. Creech, standing by the door, hasn't said anything either. I'm tired. My little girl has just woken up. This room, with its white coffin machine, is the last place we should be.

"We need to go upstairs right now." I say.

The woman in yellow looks at Creech, who says, "You heard her."

"It's protocol, Mrs. Bell."

"We can come back later."

"We can't be responsible, if there's a long wait."

"No." I say. "You can't be responsible. I'm responsible. I'm responsible for my daughter's wellbeing. And right now we need to go back upstairs, because you are terrifying her."

I sound a little shredded, even to myself, and I'm sure this is what they are thinking. But I don't

182

care.

"Dr. Patel will hear about this," says the woman in yellow. But it's a parting shot and both of us know it.

Emily says nothing on the way back up to the ICU. Her eyes are trained on me. Every time I step out of her line of vision I hear her gasp, and have to remind her that I'm still here.

Once she's settled in her room, a woman who's dressed as though she's a flight attendant comes over to us. She's carrying a clipboard and a pen and introduces herself as Leanne Mercer, the staff social worker, before turning to Emily and saying she has a few questions.

"What's your name, honey?" she asks.

"Emily Bell," says my daughter.

"Nice to meet you, Emily. Do you know where you are?"

"In a hospital"

"That's right. In the hospital. Do you know why you are here?"

"Cause my mommy says I fell."

"How did you fall, Emily?"

At this, Em turns her head and looks to me for the answer.

"It's okay, Emily," says Leanne. "Sometimes we don't remember when we fall. Now I want you to think hard. What's the last thing you remember?"

"I was in my closet," says Emily.

"In your closet? Why were you in your closet?"

"I hided from Mommy."

Leanne brushes the pen over the clipboard. "Why would you hide from your mommy, Emily?"

"Because she was bad to me."

"Did she hit you?" Leanne avoids looking at me.

I feel just about ready to hit her. Creech catches my look and puts his hand on my shoulder.

"You're not supposta hit," says Emily

"And your mommy hit you?"

Emily shakes her head.

"Are you sure?"

"Why do you keep asking me?" I can hear the strain in Emily's voice.

"Why don't you let me explain?" I don't want Emily hysterical again.

"I don't want your explanation, Ms. Prescott. I want Emily's. Emily, why were you hiding in the closet?"

"Mommy," says Emily, not pausing to glance at her. "I want to go home now."

I'm with Emily. I want to go home too. I step in and squeeze my daughter's hand and for a moment I imagine that Leanne will step between us, but she doesn't.

"We have to stay here for a while, munchkin," I say.

Emily looks like she wants to cry. "No, Mom. I want to go home. I want Chance. I want Daddy."

The pen that's been dancing ever so slightly across Leanne's clipboard stops. "Your Daddy's right here, Emily," she says.

Creech is shrinking back from the foot of the bed. God, this just keeps getting better and better. Leanne virtually stares him down. He clears his throat. "I'm not actually her father," he says, shooting me a look like we're a couple of kids who've gotten caught necking in the car.

"I can explain," I say.

"No, Mallo," says Creech. "It's my doing." His feet are shifting. I haven't seen him look this nervous since he told his dad he'd crunched the front fender when he was sixteen. "I'm not PD Bell."

"There's a surprise," says Leanne under her breath.

I'm liking her less and less.

"I'm a friend of Mallory's."

"A very close friend." I immediately regret adding this because I hear what it sounds like.

"Oh. I see," says Leanne.

I want to tell her that she doesn't see. She doesn't see at all, and even if she did see, it is none of her business. I don't say it. The water's deep enough.

"I'll be back," she says.

I can't help myself; it makes me think of "The Terminator." Leanne the terminator. It's at this point that my mother walks in carrying an oversize teddy bear.

"Grandma!" says Em.

"She's awake!" says my mother. "That's wonderful. I was so worried."

Emily makes a face. She can't seem to imagine why her grandma would be worried.

"Hello, sweetheart," my mother says to me. She puts the bear at the foot of Emily's bed and enfolds me in her arms, smoothing her hand over my back. "You must be so relieved."

Straightening, she looks Creech up and down. "Joel," she calls him by his given name as though it had gotten stuck in her mouth. I know she figures him for trouble.

Leanne is taking all of this in. I think she might be writing it down. She introduces herself to my mother. Then she tells us that the ICU allows only two visitors at a time.

She looks at Creech. "Are you a relative?" she asks.

"Not exactly," he answers.

"Then we are going to have to ask you to wait downstairs." She turns to me. "He may be your 'special friend,' Ms. Prescott, but the rules say relatives only in the ICU." She seems to be taking a perverse pleasure in telling me this.

"That isn't right," I say. I feel like punching her again, I think I'm actually considering it when Creech steps in.

"It's okay, Mallo," he says. "I'm going to go hunt down a hotel room." He looks at Leanne. "And I'll be back," he says into my ear.

I watch him walk out, thinking the whole world is nuts. My mom strokes Emily's hair, telling her she looks terrific for a little girl who fell from a tree. Leanne takes her leave. I see her talking at the station. A few of the nurses look up and glance in our direction.

"Looks like our little baby is doing real well," my mother says to me. Emily frowns. She hates being called a baby. My mother gives me another hug. Her jacket's cool from the air outside and smells of White Shoulders.

She gives me a long look, a look that says I can't possibly take care of my own life. The train wreck she predicted seven years ago has finally come to pass.

Chapter Twenty One

I could give my mother's look right back to her, but I decide not to. I'm going to ignore all the snipes and gripes and frustrations. I'm going to concentrate on getting my little girl well. The tang of bad coffee is still in my mouth.

I smile at my mom. "Thanks for coming."

"Of course I'd come, Mallory."

I wonder if I should warn her Dad's coming. My mom's a small woman, a few inches shorter than me, but she can be a force of nature. My dad, who is nearly a foot taller, is no match for her ferocity. I should pave the way, but I don't have the energy.

"Have you eaten?" my mom asks.

I think about the stale coffee cake. "Yes, just a bit ago."

"I'm hungry, Mommy," says Emily.

"Okay, sweetie. I'll see what I can do to fix that."

I haven't seen any food come or go from this place except for the tray Melissa brought for me last night. I wish Melissa were on duty now. God knows what Leanne said over at the station. I don't want to go over there and find out. But my little girl is hungry, so I go anyway and find Karen, who'd been in with us earlier.

"She's still on the IV," says Karen, walking over with me. She smiles at Emily. "You hungry, sweetheart?" Emily nods. Karen peruses Em's chart. "We should wait for Dr. Patel. Then we'll see

187

what we can do for our sleepyhead."

Emily's eyes flash between me and Karen. Lying in the crib, she looks fragile as a newborn.

"How long do you think that will be?" I ask.

"I don't know for certain. I don't imagine it will be long."

My mother sits in the chair Creech has vacated. She's wearing a three-piece ivory suit with matching ivory pumps. It's no wonder she hated Wells. In Wells, those shoes would have been mud-splattered in minutes.

My mother catches my exam and takes it for something else entirely. "I'm sure it won't be long, dear," she says. "They do like to err on the side of caution."

I sit on Emily's other side. "Grandma's right," I say "Are you very very hungry?"

"No Mommy. Just a little." She takes my hand. "If I get very very hungry, can I have some waffles?"

"Sure, munchkin." I'm ready to promise her just about anything.

Dr. Patel is with us within the half hour. He smiles at Emily and tells her that she is a very lucky girl. She tells him she wants a waffle. He chuckles, though she's dead serious.

"We have to snap some pictures of your brain first," he says. He looks to me. "They tell me they had quite a time in radiology earlier."

"I'm sorry if I caused trouble. She was just so scared."

Dr. Patel raises his little brown hand. "No need to apologize. You were quite right. Quite right."

I suck in a vindicated breath.

"I would still like the MRI done. It's important we check again for hematoma," he says.

"But she's awake." I don't want to have this

conversation in front of Emily or my mother, neither of whom will take it well.

"Yes, yes. And that is wonderful news. But these things can be very tricky. We want to be very sure."

I can't disagree with him. I, too, want to be very sure. I can't bear another trauma. Not now. I think ever so briefly about Bell.

"Okay," I say. "When?"

"The sooner the better. We will give her top priority. Number one." Then Dr. Patel tells my mother that it was very pleasant to meet her and off he goes.

My mother casts a worried glance my way. "What does that mean, hematoma?" she asks.

I ignore the question. I'm pretty sure she can figure out for herself exactly what it means.

"Here's the thing," I say to Emily, smoothing back her hair. "You took a really big tumble out of that tree in our backyard. You don't remember, I guess, but you climbed up there. And when you fell, you got knocked out. The doctor thinks you might have a bump on your brain."

I'm trying to keep it simple. It doesn't feel simple. It feels complicated and dark.

"Bumps on the brain..." I continue, "are bad things. And we need to make sure that you don't have one." Emily bites her lip as she always does when I tell her something serious. "So they need to take pictures."

"Like with a camera?"

"Not exactly." And here it comes, the hard part. "Remember the machine this morning? That was the picture machine."

Emily's shoulders curl up to crowd her ears. "No, Mommy. You said I didn't have to."

I take her hand. I'd go and do the MRI for her if I could. "I said you didn't have to right then. But you do have to now."

"You lied." She's crying again. "You said no. You said so."

The nurses look up. Leanne's still at the station. I pray she doesn't come over.

My prayer isn't answered. Leanne does come over to ask what's wrong. I'm doing my best to stay calm, but I feel like the roller coaster I've been on since I arrived here has just begun another descent.

"The MRI," I tell her. "Emily's a little scared."

My mother has taken hold of Emily's hand. She's promising waffles and teddy bears and whatever else she can think of.

"That's not unusual," says Leanne. "Is there any chance of calming her down?"

The roller coaster gains momentum. "I'm trying to do that," I say.

Leanne goes over to talk to one of the nurses. She nods and then nods again. Emily's still in the midst of a tantrum.

"You promised," she says, the tears rolling down her face. "You promised."

I've got no answer for her. Seems that most of the things I try to do for my little girl don't amount to anything.

Karen comes over with a hypodermic needle on a tray. She draws something into the shot and then pricks Emily's IV drip. "What are you doing?" I ask.

"It's a mild sedative," Karen answers.

Sixteen hours in a coma, and they are putting my child out again. This does not seem right on any level. I sit on the bed and watch the liquid drip through the tubing, powerless to stop it.

"It will help her to get through the procedure,"

says Karen. "It's okay. We do this routinely."

My little girl closes her eyes and we are right back to where we started.

An orderly comes to wheel Emily down to radiology, and I start following the crib. Karen catches my arm. "Why don't you just stay here, Ms. Prescott? She'll be out until after she gets back."

I'm swimming through too little sleep. I sit down and put my head in my hands. I'm too tired to cry. I feel my mother's hand rub my shoulder.

"Go down to the cafeteria and get yourself a decent breakfast," she says.

I fear from the tone that she won't take no for an answer.

"What if they need me?"

My mother takes my face in her hands. "Mallory, honey, you are not going to do anyone any good unless you take care of yourself." She pushes my hair back with her fingers, pulls it behind my ear. "I'll stay. I'll get you if anything happens. Now please go."

I do as I'm told, because my mother will not give me a choice. I have to give her credit. She hasn't said a word about Bell or about the whole scene with Creech. She is being extraordinarily kind, and I believe her when she says she'll come get me, though I promise myself I'll be back long before Emily is.

There's not a single unoccupied table in the cafeteria. I walk in feeling like an immigrant newly arrived on a foreign shore. Everyone's chatting. A couple sitting at a corner table hold hands. Two women dressed in scrubs laugh over something near the cashier.

I buy myself a cup of coffee. The food, under infrared light, looks indigestible. I can't stand it, this sea of people without one familiar face and I walk out, all the way out, the front entrance of the hospital.

It's cold outside. I don't have my coat and the windy March air scurries through the cotton fabric of my turtleneck and pricks my skin. I sit on the stone step, let the cold seep up through my pants and ice my thighs. I sip my coffee and wonder how long it would take me to walk home. Could I do it in a day? I think about the hill, about where I would be if I weren't here. Emily's here, and there is nowhere else for me to be. I don't want to go back to Lake Placid right now, I don't want to face the backyard. I don't want to see the tree Emily fell out of. My coffee has gone cold. I stand up, brush myself off, and head back upstairs

Emily's not back yet, but the cubicle is far from empty. My mom has been joined by my dad and the two of them are sitting very close together and talking to a third person, a middle-aged woman with short dark hair and dangly turquoise earrings.

"Mallo, honey." My dad gets to me the minute I walk in and gives me a bear-sized hug.

"What's going on?" I ask. The coffee churns in my stomach.

"I'm Vin Wagner, from State Social Services," says the woman. When she stands, she is nearly as tall as my father. "I've come to ask a few questions of little Emily, but I guess she's not available."

"Why would you want to question Emily?" I ask. Remnants of coffee rise in my throat. I should have eaten.

"I've been called in to the case by the staff here. It's fairly routine in head injury cases involving a child." Vin Wagner sits back down. She offers me the chair my father has vacated. "I'd like to ask you a few questions, too. If you don't mind."

I do mind. I mind a lot. I sit down anyway.

"You say that Emily fell from a tree?" Ms. Wagner begins. The way she says it, suggesting that it may not be the truth, angers me.

"Yes. I say that she did."

It's clear Ms. Wagner doesn't appreciate my tone. *Good.*

"Ms. Prescott, please understand we need to ask these questions."

"No, you understand." I'm back on my feet. I'm actually pointing at her. "I had the worst day of my life yesterday, followed by the worst night. And you have the balls to sit there and practically accuse me of God knows what."

My dad has his arm around me. "Mallo, you need to calm down," says my mom. She's standing too. Her hand is on my arm.

"I'm not going to calm down," I say. I'm staring hard at Ms. Wagner, wishing I could vaporize her with a look. "You have no right to come here with your allegations. What do you think—that I pushed her out of the tree?"

My dad is rubbing my arm; up and down I feel his big hand. My mom has her hand on my shoulder. "I love my little girl. What the hell is the matter with you people? I love my little girl." I'm yelling now.

I start to cry. My dad's arm pulls me close, my face is sealed against his shoulder. He smells like motor oil and coffee, same as he always has.

"As you can see, our daughter is very upset, Ms. Wagner," I hear my mother say. "She's been through a great deal."

Our daughter. I didn't think my parents shared anything anymore. But I guess I was wrong.

They share me. And Emily.

"I understand that," says Ms. Wagner. I'm a heaping mess in contrast to her calm. It makes me like her even less. "I'm just trying to ascertain the facts here. When a child sustains a serious injury, we do a report. It's routine."

I don't buy it. It is not routine. It is lack of understanding. It is being in a strange place with strangers who have no idea who you are. Who don't know you would do anything for your daughter, that you would protect her at any cost.

I inhale a deep breath and let go of my dad. I will be calm. I will have to be if I'm going to match the unsinkable Ms. Wagner. I will out calm her. "Don't let them see you sweat." It's what my dad told me about a million times in my racing days. He isn't saying it now. He looks nearly as shell-shocked as I feel.

"What, exactly, is it you want?" I ask Ms. Wagner in a tone cool enough to freeze the room.

"I want to know what happened, Ms. Prescott."

My cool is already beginning to desert me. How many times do I have to tell the same wretched story? How many times until it's as exhausted as I feel? Still, I do it.

I start with the closet, with my going upstairs to check the website. I still feel a tremor when I get to the tree. I've been over this scenario time and again. It's a film loop that won't leave my brain. You would think it would have lost its edge by now. But it has gained momentum. At this new distance, after more time has passed, I've gained perspective. The clarity makes it worse. The clarity makes it terrifying.

"What did you do after she fell?" Ms. Wagner asks.

"I covered her with my coat. I left her there to get my phone. I checked her over and called 911."

"You left her there?"

"Moving her would have been dangerous. Surely you know that, Ms. Wagner." I wasn't sure she knew. But I knew. It gives me a little bit of an edge. I knew the right thing to do and I did it. No one would fault me for my care.

Ms. Wagner takes my point. "Let's get back to the closet. Why was she in the closet?"

"She was angry with me. I don't know. She's four years old. Sitting in her closet probably seemed like a good idea."

"You didn't put her there?"

"Of course not."

"Have you ever hit Emily, Ms. Prescott?"

She's crossed a line. I refuse to answer the question.

My dad steps in. "I think that's enough. My girl wouldn't hit anybody." He looks like he would whale Ms. Wagner given the chance.

"Please answer the question, Ms. Prescott."

I clench my teeth. "No," I say, working hard to keep my voice down.

"That's all for now," says Ms. Wagner. "But I'll be back to speak with Emily when she returns."

Chapter Twenty Two

Emily's still groggy when they wheel her back into the room. There are three of us waiting for her, a clear violation of the rules, but for once nothing is said and they let us be. I stroke Emily's hair, it's oily and could use a good washing. This has been a nightmare for me. I can hardly imagine how awful it's been for my little girl.

"Mommy?" Her voice is heavy with whatever drug it is they loaded her down with. "Can we go home now?"

For about the twentieth time in the last few hours, I feel a meltdown coming on. I push it back. "Not yet, munchkin. But I'm staying right here with you. And Grandma and Gramps and Creech are here too."

I feel the omission of Bell in the pit of my stomach. The one person who should be here and isn't. I hope that Emily doesn't feel it too. If she does, she makes no comment.

Gloria comes in to check her vitals. Emily asks after breakfast again, and Gloria pretty much ignores the request. "Dr. Patel should be in soon," she says, and with that she's off.

"Mommy, my arm hurts," says Em. In all the excitement over her head, I'd forgotten about the broken arm.

"I know, sweetie. You broke it when you fell."

"I'm sorry Mommy. You told me I wasn't suppose to." She shakes her head almost wistfully.

I wonder if she'll ever climb a tree again. I

wonder if all her fearlessness has been bashed out with the fall. If I'm honest, there's a part of me that hates this thought—I want the old fearless Emily back.

We wait. Time transitions slowly from morning to afternoon. My dad walks the hall, comes back, walks out again. My mom sits in the chair. She's found an aged copy of *Good Housekeeping* in some bygone waiting room, and she's reading it word for word.

Emily is restless. To quiet her, I tell her stories. I peruse my brain for the storylines of all the bedtime books we have at home. My dad finds a store of Little Golden Books in the gift shop, and he returns with them as though they are the treasure of Sierra Madre. We read these, too.

After a while, Emily puts her hand out toward the book we've been reading and says, "Not that one, Mommy." I grab another, but she vetoes it too. "I want to hear about Daddy and the big wall." She lays back and waits.

The big wall that keeps Bell from us. That keeps him out of touch. I can almost imagine it, interrupting the phone lines. I think of the message left in the ranger station.

"Once there was a big wall," I start. My mother looks up from her magazine, then back down, trying not to be interested.

"No," says Emily. "You have to start at the beginning."

"Once there was a mountain. In a place called Alaska."

"Where it snows all the time and people live in snow houses."

"The mountain is called Denali." The sound is ruthless on my tongue.

"And there is a wall," says Emily.

My mind sails to the bivouac site, imagines a small circle of tents along the edge of a narrow ridge in a place so high the air's too thin to breathe. I imagine that protrusion of rock, the West Rib, dwarfing the encampment. I peer into the crevasse, deep and narrow and rocky, that took Roddie Kirchman's life. There is nothing but this emptiness, a mountain so big it fills the whole world. I want to be free of it, free of the stone and snow. I want to be elsewhere, in someone else's life, in another version of my own life.

"Mommy, the story," says my little girl and I know that I've stopped, mid-sentence in the telling.

"Your mommy is very tired," says my own mother.

She doesn't want me to finish the story. When she looks at me, I know she can see it to.

A big wall that stands between me and Bell. A big, big wall.

Dr. Patel brings good news. There are no obvious hemorrhages. There is no swelling. He cautions that sometimes these things can develop after an accident. And there is a tiny frontal bruise, a contusion, which may or may not cause trouble.

"We will want to keep Emily here in the hospital," he says, Emily rolling off his tongue in three lilting syllables. "We can move her to the regular pediatric wing."

I feel like we've just won the lottery. The room in the ICU makes me feel as though we're swimming in a goldfish bowl.

"And she can have some lunch, yes." He smiles at my little girl.

She looks away, suddenly shy, not sure she can trust this man.

Emily is moved to a regular room on the pediatric wing. Hers is the crib near the window. In the other bed is a baby under an air tent because she's got pneumonia. Sun shines into the room like a promise. The IV's gone from Em's arm.

An aid brings a tray with soup and a peanut butter and jelly sandwich. Emily does not like grape jelly. I coax her to eat it anyway. She manages a few bites, all the while reminding me that what she wanted was a waffle. I wonder where I can get a waffle this time of day.

"We could try the cafeteria," says my mother.

My dad takes me by the arm and says to Emily, "Your mommy and me are off to find waffles. You take care of Grandma."

He winks, at either Em or my mom, I can't be sure which, and steers me out of the room.

Breakfast ended hours ago. My dad fishes a ten out of his wallet and tells me to go get us a couple of colas. I ask the cafeteria attendant about waffles, and he tells me, just as I'd expected, that they only have waffles at breakfast. They still have Danish, he says, trying to be helpful.

"No thanks," I say. "It's waffles or nothing."

We drink the sodas. I want to hurry it up and get back to Emily. My dad seems to want to linger. After a time, I see Creech walking in the door. My father stands. He pumps Creech's hand and pats him on the back all at the same time.

"Creature," he says. "How the hell you been?" He doesn't have to feign enthusiasm. Creech has long warmed the cockles of my dad's heart. Like the son he never had.

Creech holds up a Styrofoam box. "Waffles," he

says. "Thanks to Denny's all day breakfast."

"The boy's come through," says my dad. "I knew you could do it."

"How did you know?" I asked.

"Your dad called me," said Creech. "Told me to hurry on over. His granddaughter was hungry."

"We best get this upstairs," says my dad. "Make a little girl happy."

The three of us tramp back to Pediatrics, which is way over in another wing of the hospital on the fifth floor. Not that I'm complaining. I'd like to be as far from the ICU as possible.

My mom is leaning over Emily's bed when we get there. Emily looks a little pale. She doesn't even smile when my dad announces we've got waffles.

"Mommy, I don't feel good," she says. Then she vomits the soup she's just eaten all over the front of her hospital gown.

I go out and get the nurse. Emily's still throwing up. She's crying now too. The nurse takes one look and says she'll call Dr. Patel.

"What could the problem be?" asks my mother, wiping Emily's mouth with a tissue she's extracted from her purse.

"I don't know," says the nurse.

This does nothing to reassure me.

Dr. Patel is there within minutes. He shines a penlight into Emily's eyes and checks her ears. All the while Emily's telling me that she doesn't feel good, although she has stopped vomiting. I'm holding her hand about as tight as I can. I don't want to let it go, but Dr. Patel summons me out to the hall.

"I want to do another brain scan," he says.

"What now? You just did one."

"Yes, yes. But as I told you, Ms. Prescott, these

things can be tricky. That little bruise may be swelling. And we have no time to waste."

"Fine," I tell him. "Do what you have to do." What choice do I have?

Within minutes, they've jabbed another IV into the back of Emily's hand.

She doesn't take this well. "Ow, Mommy," she says, trying to pull the hand away. "That hurts."

My mother has found some paper towels. She wets them and cleans the sick from Emily's mouth and the front of her johnny.

I pull my hand over her hair. Emily's crying and there's nothing I can do to stop it.

"We have to put her to sleep," says the nurse. She catches the look on my face. Before I can say anything, she says. "Don't worry. It's very safe."

I don't believe her.

Everyone is herded out into the hall except for me. I watch them give Emily another sedative, the second one in a few short hours. I stroke her hair and tell her everything's going to be just fine. It's a lie, and I hope she doesn't catch me in it. I don't know that anything will be fine ever again. I help wheel her out of the room and then stand there with my parents and Creech as she disappears around the corner to the elevator.

Creech is still holding the waffles. He puts his free hand to my hair. "I know this isn't the best time to tell you," he says. "But Bell called this morning."

My mom and dad both look up at the sound of Bell's name. I notice that my dad has his arm around my mom's shoulder.

"You talked to him?" I ask, feeling a little crunch, an almost anger that Creech would get to speak with him and not me.

"Yeah. They patched through." Creech's hand is still in my hair, though his eyes are on my parents. "I told him what happened. We didn't talk long."

"And?"

"And he seemed upset. He made the descent. He's coming home, though there's still a lot of snow and he didn't know when the plane would be able to get them, or even when he could get back to base."

"He wasn't at base camp."

"No. He's at second camp. Eighteen thousand feet, I think he said."

I know for a fact no one can fly into eighteen thousand feet, and he'll have to get down to base for a plane or copter to get him. If they're snowed in, who knows how long that will be.

"Mallory?" Creech is looking at me funny. I've taken hold of his arm and I'm clutching it hard.

"That's good news, honey," says my dad.

My mom doesn't say anything at all. I notice she's moved away from my father. There's a space between them now, a space that's always been there.

I let go of Creech's arm "Yes," I say. "Good news." I don't think I mean it. Not really.

The next half hour proves to be longer than it should be. We wait in Emily's vacated room. The nurse who came in earlier when Em got sick comes back to check on the baby and talk to her mom.

There are four of us crowded on our side of the room, but she says nothing about this.

"Still waiting?"

I nod, hoping for further information. "Often, it turns out to be nothing," says the nurse. "Nausea's not uncommon."

But what if it does to turn out to be something? What if they find something wrong?

"I ought to go," says Creech after the nurse leaves. I want to ask him to stay, but I can see how uncomfortable he is waiting here with my parents and me. Especially my mother, though she has said nothing about his being here. Maybe she doesn't have to. I tell him I'll walk him to the elevators.

"I'm at the Quality Inn. It's not far," he says. "Call me, if you need me for anything."

I squeeze his arm, on purpose this time. "Thanks."

He puts his hand on mine. "It's going to be okay, you know."

"How many times have you fed me that line?"

"Haven't steered you wrong yet."

And suddenly, it's as though we're back in high school. Me finding refuge in Creech. It's an old pattern.

The elevator comes and he gets on. He holds it open with his hand and looks at me with about the most serious expression I've ever seen pasted to his face.

"Anything you need, Mallo, you call me."

Impulsively, I kiss him on the cheek. I'm still feeling the scratch of his skin as the door shuts between us.

Chapter Twenty Three

I've forgotten what time is. Bell has been gone for over a month. Emily and I have been here for a day. I've been sitting and waiting for her to come back from radiology for forty-five minutes and that's the longest chunk of all. I've got way too much time to think. And the thoughts aren't good ones.

I keep thinking about Bell at eighteen thousand feet. He's so far away from us. How do I excuse his absence these past few days? He's finished the descent, done what he set out to do. Now that he's done, maybe he can turn his attention to us.

Every time I hear anything at all, I think it's Emily being brought back to the room. I've been wrong at least twenty times so far. The mom of the baby in the next bed has told me they are going home tomorrow. I'm happy for them, the baby's only two months old and nobody that small should have to endure time in a hospital. I'm also feeling the least bit envious. I wish we were being discharged tomorrow. Right now that doesn't look like it's going to happen. The baby's father rushes in. He's wearing a suit and tie and he smiles at the mom and kisses her. A little lump rises in the back of my throat and I try not to think about how far away Bell is.

My dad, who gets restless even in the best of circumstances, says he's going to go to the cafeteria for a while. More likely, he's going to walk the halls, something I'd do myself if I weren't afraid of missing

Emily's return. Even my mother is getting antsy. She keeps looking up at the clock as though it's going to divulge some great secret.

After another unbearable fifteen minutes, Dr. Patel comes in to see us. I can tell by the look on his face that the news isn't good.

He nods his head at me. "Ms. Prescott, could you come with me, please?"

I feel a knot at the base of my neck. There's a stone settling in the bottom of my stomach.

My mother looks at the doctor as though she's waiting for him to ask her to come along. Since I know she won't come of her own volition, I ask Dr. Patel for her.

"Oh yes. Certainly. By all means," he says.

He leads the way back towards radiology, which is a long way from where we are. We end up in a conference room with a backlight. Dr. Patel tacks Emily's brain scan to the light. He points to a small spot near the front of the picture.

"Can you see this?" he says, "This is what is called a hyper-dense mass."

We stare at the spot. It's a tiny little indent, barely visible. I would have missed it altogether had Dr. Patel not pointed it out.

"It's a sub-dural hematoma," he says.

The mass takes on shape and dimension. It's become a monster. I take a deep breath. I know enough about medicine to intuit what comes next.

"It looks like we have caught it quickly," says the doctor. "That is a very good thing. But it is actively bleeding."

"It will get worse," I say, not wanting confirmation.

"Yes, Ms. Prescott. It will get worse unless we go in and fix it."

"What do you mean 'fix it?'" asks my mother.

"They want to operate," I tell her. I'm surprised I can get the words out without choking on them.

"The sooner the better. We are prepping Emily for surgery, as we speak," says Dr. Patel.

Prepping for surgery. I imagine all of Emily's blonde curls sheared off. I imagine the surgeon drilling a hole into her tiny skull. It's almost enough for me to ask him to stop. Stop right now. We can't do this to a little girl. Not my little girl.

But I don't. I tell him to do what he has to do.

He puts a hand to my shoulder. "It's a small SDS," he says. "Very small, Ms. Prescott."

I nod at him, not trusting my voice.

"I will let you know as soon as there is any news." And he leaves us with the picture of Emily's brain.

It's not fair, I tell God or anyone else who might listen. She was awake. She seemed fine. It's not fair.

The nurse at the pediatric ward station tells us Emily will be transferred back to the ICU after surgery. We meet my dad in the hall by the elevator bank and my mom tells him what happened. As she talks, I feel myself start to unhinge, and soon I'm crying so hard I start to shake.

My dad puts an arm around me, squeezes my shoulder and tells me it'll be okay. In other circumstances, he would have told me to tough it out, big girls don't cry, but he doesn't do it now. People get off the elevator and walk in a wide berth around us. I wish that big girls really didn't cry. I wish I could stop.

When I do regain control, I tell my dad I have

to call Bell. Even though I know it'll be impossible to patch through, even though there's nothing he can do from three thousand miles away, he deserves to know. He stands to lose as much as I do in this.

"Honey," says my mother. "You need to worry after your own welfare. You have enough on your plate."

She's right. I've had to bear this alone so far. Why bring Bell into it now? It won't help anything.

"You can use my phone in the cafeteria," says my dad.

We find a table in the cafeteria and my mom says she's going to buy me a salad. While she's gone, I call the Talkeetna ranger station on my dad's cell. I tell them it's an emergency. This time, I'm pretty sure they hear the emergency in my voice.

They patch me through to base camp at fourteen thousand feet. There's a ranger there who tells me it's snowing hard on the glacier and Bell and his team are still up above, as far as he knows. The weather has made communication difficult. There's been some talk of them coming down early. Bell, he says, was pretty adamant about breaking camp when last they communicated. The ranger told them it would be smarter to stay put in this weather.

I give him my dad's cell number, then Creech's number again, and ask him to patch Bell through as soon as possible.

I pick at the salad. My mom thinks we should go to a motel so I can get some sleep. I tell her no a little more vehemently than I intended and end up apologizing to her.

I call Creech, but his cell's turned off. I don't

have a number for the hotel, and I can't remember where he said he was staying, so I leave a message.

"Call me," I say, and hang up before I have another breakdown.

We sit in the cafeteria for what seems like several hundred years. Sit and make small talk, though none of it really matters. My mother keeps urging me to eat, but the salad looks limp, the edges of the lettuce have already gone brown. What I do mostly is push it around the bowl.

She offers to get me something else to eat and when I say no, she gets up anyway and announces that she will get us tea. She always used to make me tea when I was sick, so she must think it helps somehow. I can't imagine it will do the trick. What I need is not tea. What I need is for my little girl to be okay.

In other circumstances, I would probably roll my eyes at my dad, the two of us sitting in judgment of Mom's nutty behavior, but I don't want to roll my eyes now. I want to close them and make this whole place disappear.

"She means well," my dad says. It occurs to me the two of them haven't fought at all in the last few hours. This is highly unusual. The two of them usually can't be in the same room together for more than five minutes without a skirmish breaking out.

"That's very generous of you to stick up for Mom."

He gives me a stern dad look. "Any trouble between me and your mother does not apply here," he says.

My mother comes back to the table with a tray and three cups of tea. She passes them out as though it were some sort of ceremony to ward off evil. I'm not crazy about tea, but I sip at it anyway, and it does have a strange sort of calming effect. Though it is not nearly effective enough.

I want to ask how much longer, but there is no one to ask except for my parents. They don't have any answers and so I spare them the grief of my question.

"I'm going to take a walk," I say, surprising myself with this new idea. I want a few minutes alone.

"I'll come along," says my mother.

"No, Mom, please. I'd rather be alone."

She looks at me, hurt. My dad puts his hand on her arm.

"You go on, sweetie. We'll wait here in case anything happens."

I leave them sitting there with the wilting salad and the cooling tea. I don't know where I'm going. I have nowhere to go. I wander down through some double doors, past patient rooms. The halls are busy. The trolley collecting food trays clatters along. An orderly wheels a patient in a wheelchair into a room. A janitor polishes the floor with a machine that whirls angrily over the tile.

I must look lost, because a nurse stops and asks if she can help me. I wish she could. There are a million questions I want to ask, none of which she can answer. I ask for a lady's room. She points back in the direction from which I came.

Just outside the double doors, there's a bank of phones with a restroom on either side. I think about calling Bell again, or Creech again, or calling Danny, but I forego the idea as useless and walk into the bathroom. And then I'm all apart again. I go into a stall and sit down. I didn't know that it was possible to cry this hard or this long. I cry for being scared of losing Emily. I cry for being scared of losing myself too. I cry for the mess I've created. It's my fault. It's all my fault. My fault and Bell's. We argued for months about his leaving. 'I told you so' doesn't cut it now. 'I told you so' doesn't change anything.

Someone knocks on the stall door and asks if I'm okay.

"Yes, fine," I manage. I catch hold of myself and wait for the other woman to leave.

My reflection in the bank of mirrors shows a woman I barely recognize. There are dark circles under my swollen red eyes. My whole face is puffy.

"You look like hell, Mallory," I tell the reflection. And then I tell the sagging woman in the glass that she'd better get hold of herself.

I splash some cold water on my face. There aren't any paper towels, only air dryers. *It figures.*

I look at my reflection again and promise things will get better.

The woman in the mirror stares back. She doesn't believe me.

Chapter Twenty Four

Creech is sitting with my parents in the cafeteria. He looks like he's just woken up. My father's hand is on Creech's shoulder. My mother has her arms folded, her mouth tucked down against the environment or Creech or both. They don't see me.

I breathe in deep, aware of the big strides I'm trying to take across the slick, waxed cafeteria floor. Like skating, I think, only not as graceful. I tell myself to be brave. I tell myself I know how to do this. I think about my dad, my first coach, and have a sudden vision of the start house at the top of the Ridge trail at Ridge Run.

I'm eight years old and the course is in rough shape. Deep ruts between gates glisten with ice. My heart is beating too fast. "Be brave, girl," says my father. "Nothing to it. You're bigger than the run, that's what you've got to remember." I push the start wand with my thigh. A cold rush of wind slaps against me, and I forget everything except the next turn, the next gate.

Be brave, I tell myself. You're bigger than this thing. But I don't feel bigger. The ice wind has been traded in for the peculiar smell of cafeteria food left to congeal under infrared light. I'm not bigger. I'm not anyone at all. This is how we fall. This is how we get hurt.

Creech comes over when he catches sight of me. He can see I'm struggling, and he's ready to grab me and save me from falling. Only he can't see that it's impossible to grab me. Like on those long-ago runs down the hill, I'm the only one who can keep myself from crashing the gate.

He plants a kiss on the top of my head, and together we walk back to the table. I watch my mother's frown deepen. I worry for a minute she'll say something, but she doesn't. I'm conscious of my hand in Creech's as we sit. The warmth of his fingers is needed and I'm not willing to drop it.

The food is gone, and I'm glad I don't have to look at it anymore. My mother looks at me as though I've just returned from some epic journey. She looks to see if I've changed. Maybe she wonders if I've finally come to my senses after a seven-year hiatus. Maybe she hopes when this is all done, I'll straighten out the mess I've made of my life. I know there is no going back, but I do wonder. Where would I be if I'd stayed in Albany and married Tommy Nussman like I was supposed to? I'm guessing I wouldn't be here.

Creech, maybe becoming aware of my mother's look, has dropped my hand. He stands up and asks if anyone's up for coffee. I don't want any. Neither does anyone else. I go with him to the cook station anyway. I can't just sit and wait for the train to derail. Coffee, it seems, is a better option.

The coffee we get is old and cold enough that the powdered creamer I pour into it clumps into scummy islands that bob on the surface. The whole world feels like it's clumping into some sort of surreal landscape, a dream I wander through without knowing how to wake myself.

I walk outside of myself; watch myself as I walk back to the table with Creech. I could float away like so much ash. Then I think of Emily, and I'm back to being stuck inside the hard, sterile walls of the hospital, helpless to do anything besides wait. The waiting takes hours, time burns slowly leaving its charred remains. I don't know time anymore, can't tell if it's passing or not.

Dr. Patel appears at the door wearing oft-laundered scrubs. He looks as tired as I feel. In other circumstances, I might feel sorry for him, but right now all I feel is a mounting impatience at how long it takes him to come over to us.

He tells me Emily has come through the surgery well. "She is in recovery," he says. "Then we will need to move her back to the ICU."

I have the urge to kiss him, but I shake his hand and thank him instead. I dread going back to the ICU. I do not want to see Leanne again. I hope she won't be there. I'm hoping, in fact, she's no longer on staff here. A trolley of trays jostles by and I'm distracted again. I can't seem to keep my head on any one thing anymore.

"Honey, you look tired," says my mother. The elastic in her smile is loosened around the corners.

"I can get a cot in the ICU," I say, though I'm not at all sure I can. I'm not sure of anything anymore.

My clothes stick to me. I've been in them since we came. Since the morning before we came. I think back to shoveling the drive, Emily dressing herself. It seems like weeks ago, another lifetime, another life I'm not living anymore and I'm not sure I can ever get back to.

My mom and I go up once Emily's back in the ICU. I thought I'd be relieved to see her, but there she is looking as though she's in a coma again. They haven't shaved her hair, at least not all of it, and it sticks out unruly from under the wide bandage that circles her head. Her skin, normally rosy, looks transparent as bone china. The sight of her starts my tears all over again, and I collapse into the chair next to the crib and put my head in my hands. I feel my mother's hand running along my hair.

"You need to rest," she says.

She goes off and leaves me alone with the hums and beeps of Emily's monitors. I keep telling myself to pull it together. The worst is over. Dr. Patel said the surgery went well. Everything is going to be okay. I repeat this to myself over and over, as though repeating it will guarantee it's true. I think maybe I fall asleep, because the next thing I know, my mother is back with an orderly, showing him where to put the cot he's wheeling into the room. He sets it up and my mother tells me to lie down on it.

"Take off your shoes," she says.

I do as I'm told. I lie down and my mother tucks me under the blankets as though I'm the one who's four years old.

The last thing I remember before falling asleep is my mother's hand on my forehead like she's checking for fever.

When I wake up there's no way of telling whether it's day or night. My hair is matted to my head; my teeth are knit together by a wretched tasting film. Emily is asleep or out, I don't know which. A nurse I've never seen before comes in to check on her.

"Is it morning? I ask, feeling stupid I don't have such basic information.

"Yes, it is. Is there anything you need?"

The film on my teeth feels thick enough to bottle. "Could I get a toothbrush?"

"Of course." A few minutes later she comes

back with toiletries in a plastic kidney-shaped dish and tells me there's a bathroom just down the hall from the ICU.

In the bathroom, I wash my face in the sink and run a small black comb through my tangled hair. I feel like a homeless person living in an airport terminal. There's a banging pain in my temples. I walk back down the hall, sit on the cot, and wish that I could go back to sleep.

I lie down and close my eyes. My mind drifts off to Bell and, because it's all too tender to think about the snow on Denali and where he might be, I get up again and watch Emily sleep. I wonder how long she'll be out. They assume she's fine, but she doesn't look fine to me. She doesn't look like Emily at all.

There's a knock on the glass and there's my father standing just outside the door. He hesitates to come in, as though this were my adolescent bedroom, a place he can't enter without my expressed permission. I've not thought much about my father's age before, but as I watch him take Emily's tiny hand into his own big one, I notice how his hair has grown spare along his forehead. How small wrinkles have begun to run fracture lines over his face.

"How did you sleep?" he asks after a time, as though it had finally occurred to him what to ask.

I tell him that I slept okay, realizing for the first time that I did. I tell him I feel a little grungy. "Like camping without the woods," I say.

His face breaks into a tired smile. "Remember that old tent we bought you, what was it, your tenth birthday? We set that thing up in the yard. Rained like a son-of-a-gun, but you insisted on sleeping out there. By yourself." He shakes his

215

head. "I must've gotten up four times that night, just to make sure you hadn't floated away."

The closed humid interior of the tent comes back to me. I'm breathing in the rain-soaked air. I'd wanted to go back into the house so badly, but I could never have lived with myself if I had. Even then, I'd been stubborn as hell. I learned to love that tent. I spent a good part of the summer sleeping in it.

"I still have that tent," I tell my dad, "It's out in our garage somewhere."

"No kidding?" He puts his fingers to Emily's bandage, touching it as though it might break.

The garage makes me think of home. I wonder if Creech shut off the lights. I wonder if I left the heat on. It doesn't really matter. The place is empty. Bell's not there and neither is Emily. It pains me to think of it as deserted.

"Creech is downstairs. He drove over with me." There's a little question mark in my dad's eyes when he mentions Creech to me.

"He's a good friend. The best."

"You've been friends a long time," says my dad, and then he pauses as though to say something else. "Anyway, he doesn't want to come up here after all the fuss."

"Poor Creech, I should really tell him he should go home."

"But you're not going to."

I think about this. I should let him go, but I can't. I need him here.

"I'm not surprised to see him." Dad doesn't explain further, as though his meaning should be evident.

"Bell hasn't called?" I ask, changing the subject. I know the answer. My dad would have told me if he had.

"No. Why don't you go down and have breakfast with Creech? I'll sit with our girl. Your mom will be by soon. She was taking a shower when I left."

This stops me. "You and Mom shared a room?"

"It's a little cheaper that way," says my dad.

"Wow," I say.

"It's not such a big deal, Mallory. Don't make something out of nothing, okay?"

"Okay," I say, but it really does feel like a big deal to me.

Chapter Twenty Five

The cafeteria is crowded this morning, making it seem a whole different place than it was last night. I don't see Creech anywhere and then suddenly feel a hand on my shoulder and there he is standing right next to me. He's clean-shaven and has on a fresh chambray shirt that's wrinkled around the collar.

"How's Emily?" he asks.

"Not awake," I answer, trying to shrug off the nagging worry that her not being awake causes me. "They tell me she's doing well, though I haven't talked to Dr. Patel yet."

I smile. Maybe if I can do that, I can make it all better. People skirt us on their way to the cook station. "Dad says you'll buy me breakfast."

Creech puts his arm around me and steers me towards the line waiting for food. "Anyone ever tell you you're a mooch?" He puts a tray on the rail in front of us. I pick up a bagel and some cream cheese. He takes an egg sandwich, and then adds a yogurt, two bananas and two coffees. He pays for the whole thing, and I let him.

I'm surprised by how good the bagel tastes. I really haven't eaten since we got here and I guess I'm a little hungry. Creech watches me devour the thing, his sandwich half gone.

"Adam called last night," he says. "He's leaving for Alta today. He asked after you. Said to tell you he was sorry."

I nod, wondering if Adam is sorry about what

happened to Emily or what happened between us. I don't want to go there, not ever again. He's got a life to get back to, and he'll put it all behind him soon enough. If he hasn't already. Creech has a life to get back to, too. I'm keeping him here in suspended animation, and I'm a lot guiltier over this than my near miss with his brother.

"What about you?" I ask. "What about work?"

Creech shrugs. "It's the end of the season. I've got some time coming. Don't worry about it."

"I do worry about it. I don't want you..." I drop off, not sure how to put it. I don't want you putting yourself out is what I'd wanted to say, but that doesn't seem right.

"What, Mallo?"

"I don't know. I don't want you to lose your job or something."

Creech laughs. "That's not going to happen. I was going to take some time anyway. I'm going to go up to Wells for a while. Go fish in the Sacandaga, take the kayak out once the ice is gone." He bites his lip, an old habit that lets me know he's thinking on something. "I've got some choices I need to make."

"What kind of choices?"

"Nothing for sure. Nothing I want to talk about just yet. Anyway, it's not so important. What's important is getting Emily out of here. So I'm going to hang around a while, okay?"

He squeezes my hand, then hands me the banana and tells me to eat it. "It's got potassium and other good stuff in it," he says. I eat the banana and the yogurt. "You look better already," he says.

"Was I that bad?"

"You are never that bad."

"I feel hugely grungy. I don't have a change of clothes. I think I'm going to ask my mom to get me something. She loves to shop." I consider the clothes my mother would buy for me and picture myself in a calico print dress with a lacy collar and matching pastel pumps. "Or maybe not. God, she'll try to dress me up like church on Sunday."

"And that would be bad because why?"

"It just would."

Creech leans back in his chair and studies me, the dimple in his cheek showing. "I think you'd look terrific in a dress, Mallo."

"You got a problem with the way I dress?" I say to cover my discomfort at the way he's looking.

He looks away. "No," he says. "You dress fine. I'm sorry I said anything." He stares at me again, the corners of his mouth pucker. "You look just fine."

I leave Creech sitting in the cafeteria with a promise to come down later. Leanne is standing by the elevator bank. I'd like to avoid her and I think about taking the stairs, but I'm going to have to deal with her sooner or later, so I walk up and say hello as politely as I can muster.

"Ms. Prescott," she says. "How is Emily?"

"All right," I say. "Better."

"That's good." We get on the elevator together, its sole occupants. I stand as far away from her as I can without being obvious.

Leanne faces me, "Perhaps we need to clear the air," she says.

I straighten, waiting for the next confrontation and wishing hard I'd reconsidered the stairs.

"I'm sorry if..." The elevator doors open and

220

she stops.

I fold my arms and wait for them to shut again.

"I'm sorry if we upset you, Ms. Prescott. It's protocol. It's my job. You'll be pleased to hear we called Adirondack Medical and Dr. Ferris gave you a glowing recommendation."

"Did he tell you that Emily fell?"

"Ms. Prescott—"

I don't allow her to finish. "I suggest, Ms. Mercer, you investigate before you start throwing accusations around. You could save people a lot of grief, if you did. Or is that not your job?"

The elevator stops on the fifth floor, two floors above the ICU. I get off before she can answer. I walk the two flights down. I have the energy to do it now.

There are voices in the lounge next to the ICU. Familiar voices arguing. I knew the room share was a bad idea. I'm surprised my parents have held it together as long as they have. The argument is more civil than some I've experienced in the past, I'll give them that much. No one is shouting, or throwing anything, or slamming doors. I hear my name and then Creech's. My mother says something about 'inappropriate.' My father answers with a rumble too low to register the words. I come around the corner making a goodly amount of noise, so they'll know I'm here. Just like in my teens, the conversation freezes and the two of them bound over towards me.

"Did you eat?" asks my mother.

"Doctor's with Emily," says my father at the same time. "She's awake."

"Why didn't you come get me?" I'm a little upset Em woke up and I wasn't there.

"We knew you'd be along soon enough. And here you are." My mother says this as though it's a big surprise I'm here.

"I'm going to go see my daughter. I'll leave you two to whatever you were discussing." I say this in a way I know I might regret later, but I'm ticked enough not to care.

When I enter Emily's room, Dr. Patel is asking her to put her pointer fingers together. He steeples his own fingers to demonstrate. Then he touches his nose and asks Emily to touch hers.

Emily follows the directions easily, though she stops when she sees me. "Mommy," she says, "Where were you?" adding to my already guilty conscience.

"Just getting some breakfast, sweetie."

The doctor gives Em a wink and tells her that he needs to talk to Mommy for a minute. We step outside the glass.

"We are very lucky," he says. "No outward signs of impairment. She seems to have sailed through the surgery."

This sounds grand in his singsong voice. I wait for a caution light. There always seems to be one. But the only thing he says is, "Another set of pictures in a few days to be certain. After that she will be ready to go home."

"So soon?" I wonder aloud. I think about my empty house, about the tree in the yard. For all my wanting to get out of here, I'm not sure I'm ready to go back home just yet.

Dr. Patel leaves and I am left alone with my daughter. I apologize to Emily for not being there when she woke up. I'm feeling very contrite. I'm feeling like I might not leave her bedside again, though I know this is impossible. I want to attach her to me so nothing bad will ever happen to her again, but this is even more impossible.

My mom comes back without my dad. Emily and I are playing "Thumkin" to pass the time. I keep waiting for Emily to bring up her daddy, but so far she hasn't said a thing about him. I tell my mom I could use some clothes. "Sweats," I say. "Preferably blue or black." I sound like an adolescent brat. My parents' fighting has started to make me feel that way.

"A little color wouldn't hurt, you know," my mother says. I have images of lime, fuchsia, magenta; my mother's idea of sprucing up.

"Blue, Mom. And what were you and Dad arguing about?"

"Discussing. And we can talk about it later."

She tucks the corner of Emily's blanket under the mattress with some deliberation. Emily watches both of us. I figure I should stop the bickering while I can. "Thanks, Mom. For being here. For everything."

"You're certain you want blue?" she says, coming out with a peace offering of her own.

Two days pass and we are out of the ICU. Emily's head and arm are getting progressively better. I spend the time eating, sleeping, and sitting. Mostly sitting. The routine here has become my own. I mark time by the nurses coming and going. There's time to think. I spend a lot of time thinking. Nights are the worst. Emily sleeps and I toss on the cot. The thought reels that loop through my brain are always the same: Where is Bell? Why hasn't he called? Why aren't I a better mother?

Time is punctuated by meals and visits. My

mother and father take turns sitting vigil. Now that the crisis is over, I really want for them to go home, though of course I can't tell them that. Creech left yesterday. There wasn't much sense in his hanging around anymore. He's gone to Wells to stay with his folks for a few weeks.

Wells sounds like an oasis to me. A step backwards to the place where I used to live before I met Bell and we built a house and had a little girl who fell from a tree. I was happy there, in that life, despite the bickering of my parents. I was happy with winters spent at Ridge Run and summers at the lake nearby or climbing through the local hills with Creech and the band of friends we used to hang with. Sometimes it doesn't seem all that long ago, weeks instead of twelve or fifteen years. When I talked to Creech earlier this evening, and he told me how the Sacandaga River was running hard and wild with all the rain they've had the past week, how the trails along the ridge were mucky wet, I felt a kind of homesickness for that easier time. I keep thinking a step back may be just the sort of medicine I need.

When my dad comes in after dinner I climb around the idea of home. "You know that visit?" I ask.

He looks blank. So much has happened since we talked about my visiting him that he doesn't seem to remember it.

"Me and Emily coming to see you?"

"Oh, sure." He looks pleased I'm making plans past the hospital. "In a couple of months it will be warm enough to swim."

"I was thinking sooner. Like when we get out of here tomorrow."

He doesn't answer right away. I know he's

thinking I ought to get back to my own house. I have Bell to consider. But I haven't heard from Bell in days. And every time I think about home, I watch Emily tumble from the maple tree in the backyard.

Finally, he says, "You're welcome to stay with me any time, sweetie. If you're sure it's what you want."

"For a little while," I say, though this is not the truth. The truth is I want to take Emily and live in my father's house for as long as I can.

Emily is asleep. She's always been a champion sleeper, but here she's sleeping long even by her standards. I pick up the Vermont Bear the crew from work sent. He's on crutches, his leg and head swathed in bandages. A 'Get Well Soon, Emily' card is slung around his neck, signed by all the guys on the patrol, even Turk. I look at a note for me from Albie saying I can take all the time I need. Albie's being sweet, I know, but the note makes me feel like they don't need me. The place is running along just fine without me. Which is both what I want and what I don't want.

My mom comes in with a Target bag. Since I asked for sweats, which she purchased in a pale sky blue, she's been to the store twice. Today she unwraps a pink sweater, a pair of jeans, and another package of underwear. It's like I've given her a license to shop. "A few things to make you feel better," she says.

When I tell her about my plans to visit Dad after Emily's discharged, her smile fades and she looks at me like I've finally lost my mind. I quickly amend my plans. "We'll come visit you, too. If you'd like."

"I'd love to have you, Mallory," she says. "But that's hardly the issue." She casts an accusing glance at my father, a look that says he's done it again, enough to make him fold his arms and glance toward the door.

Since my dad won't offer up two words in his defense, I tell my mom I invited myself to stay with my father, just so she'll know.

She shakes her head at me and says, "Oh, Mallory," in a way that says I've messed up big time.

"I need a little time away. And I love Wells," I say, on the defensive for myself now.

"And Joel Crèches will be there," she says, none too kindly.

"Jean," my father says in a 'don't go there' tone. A tone my mom and I are both pretty familiar with and one she usually ignores. As she does now.

"God knows I don't always agree with the choices you make, Mallory," she says. "But please don't try to rectify one bad choice with another."

"What is that supposed to mean?" I say, overriding my father who has said "Jean" again and looks like he'd like to drag my mother out of the room by whichever arm he can grab first. My mother ignores him still.

The bed next to Emily's is empty. I'm really glad there is no one else here to witness this outburst, not the first and probably not the last in this family.

"You know very well what I mean, Mallory," says my mother. "Trust me on this, Joel Crèches is not a refuge."

I feel a sharp anger rise in my throat. How dare she deride Creech after all his kindness. His friendship means the world to me. I'm ready to blast her out of the room.

My dad steps between us. "Jean," he says. His

voice has gone up a decibel. "That's enough."

Emily stirs and opens her eyes.

"That's lovely, Harry. Wake your granddaughter." She goes over to Emily's bed as though she's defending it. My father starts looking contrite.

"That's it," I say. "I want you both to leave. Right now."

"Really, Mallory," says my mom. "If we can't discuss things like rational adults—"

"I'm not defending Creech to you or anyone." I almost tell her that it's none of her business, but I stop myself. She may never speak to me again, if I do.

"Mommy?" says Emily.

I give both my parents an exasperated look. "I'm right here, baby. Grandma and Gramps were just leaving. Say goodnight, okay?"

I've trumped them here. There is nothing either of them can do. My mother kisses Emily's forehead and throws me a killer glance before making her exit. My father hangs back a minute and watches her go.

"I'm sorry I woke her up," he says to me before kissing Em goodnight. "Buck up, kiddo," he tells her. "You'll be out of here tomorrow." Then he turns to me. "You come on up. Stay as long as you want."

With this, we are sealed, like we always were. Co-conspirators, my father and I, against my mother's notion of how the world ought to be.

I give him a kiss on the cheek. "Thanks, old man." I watch him go out the door and then we're alone again, just Emily and I.

Emily yawns. I stroke her hand. "Go on back to sleep, munchkin." I watch as she drifts off, her little face made smaller by a hat of bandages. "I'll

227

take care of you forever," I say, though she is already fastened back into her dreams.

The place has gotten quiet; the only sound in the room is the hum of a florescent light that shines over Emily's head. I shut this off, and the room goes dark. The only light comes in through the window. This light, like florescence, is artificial, made of streetlights and traffic lights and car lights reflected on wet pavement. I go to look at it, but there is not much of a view; just the roof of another wing of the hospital one floor below, a silver fan housed in a corner. Beyond is a half-filled parking lot and beyond that the highway. Still, I gaze at it as though it were the view from my back porch, as if hemlocks were lined along the ridge underlining the mountains beyond them. I miss that view. I'll miss that view.

A voice comes up behind me, startling me, because it's straight from those far off hills. "Mallory?"

I turn to see him. Bell, standing at the foot of Emily's bed.

Chapter Twenty Six

He looks as though the Alaska Mountains have leaned hard on him. His collarbone sticks out like a hanger for the T-shirt he wears. His eyes, usually bright enough to catch me up, sag heavy over deep lines.

I'm gathered into him before I have the chance to say anything at all. He smells of sweat; I imagine how many hours he's spent crumpled in an airplane seat. For a minute, I want all time to end here.

He kisses my forehead, and I burrow into the hollow of his arm. We stand there for an endless amount of time, until he lets go and walks over to Emily and fingers the bandage on her forehead. The air between us accordions out. Three thousand miles are still there, in the narrow space between the window and the bed.

"How is she?" he asks.

"We get discharged tomorrow."

I think about how much Bell's absence has cost me, has cost both of us, and I can't look at him.

"I'm glad she's coming home tomorrow," he says, sounding terrible and contrite.

I can't do it. I can't go home and pretend none of this ever happened. I want to. I want to so badly it makes me hurt. But I can't. Not yet. Maybe never.

"We're not going home," I tell him.

He pulls his hand from Emily's forehead as though the bandage has suddenly gotten hot.

229

"Why?"

"I can't. I can't face the house. I can't face the tree." I say all this to the window. Five floors below a car pulls from a parking space. The ground is slick. It has begun to rain. "I'm going to Wells to stay with my dad."

"Mallory?" There is a question in his voice, a hint of alarm.

"I can't do it. I'm sorry. I can't keep hanging in while you leave us."

Bell's come close again. His hands are on my shoulders. "I never left you, Mallo. I would never leave you or Emily. I love you. I love her. She's my kid, too."

He pulls me around and when he looks me in the eye, I see a pain cross his face, something bright and searing enough to make him drop his hands.

"I moved the world to get here. I would do it again."

"It wasn't soon enough." I'm crying hard now.

Bell backs away. He stops to touch Emily's hand, he strokes it, and then he's out the door.

I have a thousand rejoinders to hurl after him. I want to tell him he ought to take some responsibility for once. Or to tell him that he's always walking away and why should now be any different.

But the biggest part of me wants to tell him to stay. For once, please just stay.

I spend a fretful night on the cot, dissecting the scene with Bell, playing it over, changing it, and I'm out of sorts when Dr. Patel shakes my hand the next morning. He doesn't seem to notice. He's all smiles as he gives me a list of precautions and tells me I have to bring Emily to see him late next week. I wish I were in a better mood to receive his optimistic outlook.

Emily wakes up soon after he leaves. I hate myself for it, but I don't tell her Bell was here. I tell myself it will be easier if she doesn't know just yet. I do remind her we are going to Grandpa's. I talk on for a bit about Coot, my dad's old blue tick hound and about how great the hill is and the river is. I tell her we'll have a wonderful time, and she's so excited to go that she wants to skip breakfast when it comes.

My mom is not so easy to fool. She comes in soon after breakfast and immediately asks me what's wrong. I tell her nothing, but I can see she doesn't believe me.

She turns to Emily and says; "I hear a little girl is getting out of the hospital today."

Emily repeats all I said about Coot and Grandpa's place.

My mother says, "Isn't that nice," but she's looking at me as though her fondest wish is that I'll change my mind and I know, if not for Emily, I'd be getting an earful.

My dad comes in at ten to pick us up. We're all set to go, our few belongings packed in two grocery sacks. My mom unveils a new dress, two pairs of pants, and a shirt she bought for Emily. My dad takes one bag and I take the other. An orderly arrives with a wheelchair and Emily gets into it and the whole caravan departs for the lobby. My mom questions me about what the doctor said for the fourth time and then spouts advice all the way to the elevators.

When the doors open in the lobby, Emily

jumps from the chair. "Daddy," she yells loud enough to turn heads. "Daddy! Daddy!"

Bell stands up from a lobby chair looking startled and then squats down and gathers our little girl into his arms. He's wearing the same clothes he had on last night. I wonder if he spent the night in the lobby. It wouldn't surprise me, if he had.

"I felled from a tree," Emily tells him.

"I heard about that," he says.

My parents and I walk towards him and we circle each other like a cluster of mutes.

Finally, my dad offers Bell his hand. "Good to see you, Bell."

Bell stands, taking Emily up with him, and shakes my father's hand.

My mother finally blinks. She looks from me to Bell and Emily to my father. "I'm going to be on my way. It's a long drive to Albany." She gives me a big hug. "You take care of yourself," she says, raising an eyebrow.

"Yes, sure. See you soon."

She gives Bell a long sour look before putting her hand to Emily's shoulder. "Be a good girl for Mommy." She kisses her forehead. I notice she's careful not to touch Bell. She does manage to say, "It's good to see you again, Peter." And the two of them smile warily at each other.

"I'll walk you out," my father says. I imagine it's as much to escape an awkward situation as it is anything else.

My mother does not let him off the hook. "I can see myself out, Harry," she says. Although she does kiss him on the cheek. We watch as she walks out, her heels tapping against the hard floor.

"Did you ski down the big wall, Daddy?" Emily

asks Bell.

"Yeah, baby, I did." He looks more as though he'd survived a shipwreck than conquered a mountain.

"Good for you, Daddy!"

Bell smiles at her, a smile that doesn't carry over into his eyes.

He looks at me for a long minute and then smoothes back Em's hair. "You and Mommy are going to Grandpa's, I hear." He says this softly, like it's hard for him to get the words out.

"You can come too, Daddy. We're going to see Coot."

Bell looks at me again. I'm reminded of freeze tag, a game I used to play as a kid. Touch me and I can't move. Only Bell isn't touching me. It's his eyes. His eyes are more than touching, they are pounding me. Hard.

"I can't do that right now, Munch," he says, making his voice casual.

"How come?"

I can hear the disappointment. It hits me hard too. One more blow and I'll be on the floor.

"Because I've got to go home and take care of some stuff," he says. I can see how the lie gets caught in his mouth.

"Then I can come with you," says Emily.

"No, baby," I say, my own words stuck to the roof of my mouth.

"But I want to stay with you, Daddy."

My own father starts digging into his pocket and draws out his car keys. "I'll meet you outside," he says.

I nod at him, not trusting my voice.

Bell tries to put Emily down, but she clings tight to his neck. He finally gives up and pulls her in tight.

"Emily and I are going for a walk, okay?" he says to me.

They walk off down the hall, and it's my turn to sit. I watch people go in and out of the lobby. Ten minutes pass, then fifteen. My mom's long gone. My dad will wait, though I know he won't come back in. I have a vision of me going without Emily. It leaves me cold.

When they finally do come back, Emily's walking under her own power, though her hand is still firmly clasped in her father's.

"Okay, Mom," she says. "We can go now."

She sounds for all the world like she's resigned to my dragging her off to prison camp somewhere. I follow them out to the parking area, where my dad has the car running. Bell puts Emily in the car seat, kisses her forehead. "I'll see you soon, Emily. You have fun with Grandpa and Mommy."

She nods at him. "I love you, Daddy," she whispers.

"I love you too, munchkin," he says. When he ducks out of the car, I can see the strain on his face.

"I just need some time," I tell him. I'm not sure this is true. We've been apart for six weeks and time has solved nothing.

"I can give you time," he says, shoving his hands into his pockets. "You know where to find me."

He stands on the curb as we drive off. I watch him shrink into the distance.

Wells is a good distance from Burlington, made longer by the hushed silence in the car. My father has always been a quiet man, and he says very little now. Emily isn't talking either. When I look back at her she's staring out the window.

I turn on the radio to try and lighten the mood, but only succeed in filling an empty hole with noise. I'm enormously relieved when we get to Wells and turn up the access road to Ridge Run. I haven't been home in what seems a very long time, but the place is still as familiar as my own backyard.

My dad's house is near the foot of the access road. The front yard faces north and is still covered in snow. The sun's done work on the south-facing ski slope though. The snow's spotty at best. Even from the house, you can see large rocks protrude, and the weeds and grass at the base of the chair towers are already green.

The weather's been warm. It's up around fifty degrees today. My dad catches me looking up at the hill as we pull into the drive.

"Whole new generation of little kids tearing through the snow up there now," he says.

My room looks much the same as it did when I left home to go to college; only it's neater. There's a shelf loaded with ski trophies from as far back as the fourth grade and a full size trail map of Ridge Run tacked to the wall. The dresser is overflowing with snapshots I framed myself when I was in high school. There's one of me and my dad, taken back when I was fourteen or so, standing in the start house up on the mountain. There's another of Creech and me in our early teens mugging for the camera on the veranda of the base lodge. I pick it up. We were so young then: Creech with his hair cut short, a cowlick sticking up in the front, me in braces.

My dad brings the old cot into my room and

235

puts it next to the single bed. "You sure you want to sleep on this old thing?" he asks Emily, who has come up behind him.

"Yes," she says. There's no hemming and hawing in that girl. I put the picture down and my dad glances at it. He doesn't say anything, and I guess I'm grateful he doesn't.

Later, after we've downed a quick supper of macaroni and cheese and turkey sandwiches, my Dad asks the question that I know has been niggling at him all day. "So, Mallo. How long you plan on staying?"

Em's off watching TV in the living room. Coot's head is parked in her lap. She's scratching his ears and telling him something and he looks for all the world like he's listening. I point this out to my dad, because I don't know how to answer him. He smiles at his granddaughter and his dog, but he is not so easily put off.

"It's not that I mind you being here, sweetie," he begins as he stacks bowls into the dishwasher.

I pick up the last two glasses and put them in. My dad will stop asking, I know, if I keep ignoring him, but he deserves better than that.

"I don't know, Dad. How long can you stand me for?"

He smiles at this and asks if I want coffee.

"Sure."

He measures out two mug fulls and pours milk into each.

We sit out on the front porch step, bundled in jackets. It's a clear night, a million stars blanketing the sky. Light from the TV flickers through the window. The ridge looms in front of us. I think about Bell, how he would know the names of all the constellations, and the thought leaves me raw with

236

missing him.

"So, Creech has gone north until tomorrow," says my dad, sipping at his cup.

"Yeah. He has some kind of a meeting he had to go to. He's being pretty mysterious about it."

My dad's teeth gleam in the semi-darkness. "Guess I never thought Creech was mysterious," he says.

I laugh. It's true. Creech is not the kind of guy to keep a secret. Creech will tell you what he got you for your birthday three days before he gives it to you. But in this, he's playing his cards close to his vest. It makes me wonder what's up.

"Think he'll give up his job and come work with us?" my dad asks.

"I can't imagine. He loves his job. He's good at it too."

"He was one hell of a racer. Shame what happened to him."

I nod, though I doubt Creech would call it a shame. He would say it is what it is. He's always been good at dealing with whatever life hands him.

My dad glances up at the mountain. "Some of us are just better at playing those hands," he says. "You and I, we have a lot to learn."

He looks at me, another man being mysterious when he's usually not. "I don't mean to criticize, baby. But you coming here licking your wounds, well, that's okay for a time. But sooner or later you're going to have to face down whatever it is that's going on between you and Bell."

He sounds an awful lot like my mom, who is always doling out advice. My dad is not in the habit of giving any sort of counsel though. And coming from this new perspective, I can see his point. I am hiding out.

I turn my cup around in my hands. "I told Bell I needed some time." I look out to the ridge. Dark contours shift in the moonlight. "And he told me to take the time."

My dad pats my knee. "You'll figure it out, Mallo. You've always been good at figuring out what you need."

"That's not what Mom thinks."

"Guess she and I see things different. But I'll tell you this too, Mallo. You're no quitter. You're a fighter. Don't go quitting now."

He kisses my head and gets up. "It's been a long day. I'm going to turn in."

It's only around eight o'clock, but I know what he means. "Goodnight then."

"Goodnight, sweetie. Don't stay out too long"

And he leaves me sitting out on the step, sipping on his words.

Chapter Twenty Seven

I wake up to find the cot next to my old single bed empty. I panic until I realize that it's bright outside and long past the middle of the night. I scoot into my clothes and go downstairs. There's no one around and the clock in the kitchen shows it's after one. I can't believe how late it is. I went to bed at nine, meaning I slept for sixteen hours straight.

I hear a noise and there's Dad with Emily up on his shoulders coming around the side of the house.

"Hey, sleepyhead," he says, when he steps through the door.

"Where have you been off to?"

"We walked over to John and Marie's." The Crèches' house is a quarter mile down the road. "Wanted to show off my granddaughter."

I don't like that he'd just taken off with Emily, even though they hadn't gone far. "I wish you'd told me."

"Figured you needed the rest. And I did leave a note." My dad points to a scribble attached by magnet to the fridge.

Emily has begun running circles around the kitchen with Coot, who was also a part of this morning's expedition.

"Slow down," I tell her. The kitchen counters have sharp edges. I see re-injury everywhere, but Emily is not about to slow.

"Whoa," says my dad, catching her up again. "How's about we make some lunch?" He pulls out a

239

loaf of bread and some peanut butter. Emily makes a face. "What's wrong?" asks my dad.

"I don't like peanut butter," says Emily.

"Your mom loves peanut butter. For about three years, that's all she ate." He looks at me and winks. "How's about we make her a sandwich?"

Emily likes this idea and pretty soon she's got two slices of bread and she's glopping peanut butter all over both with a butter knife. When she flips the slices together, the stuff's hanging out off the side.

"Here, Mommy."

I take a bite though I'm not really hungry. "Mmm, yummy. Some coffee would really go good with this sandwich," I say, hunting for filters.

My dad eyes me as I fill the carafe with water. "Sleep did you good, Mallo."

"You're the one who's Mr. Cheer."

"What's not to cheer? I got the two prettiest girls in the world staying with me."

I can see that he is genuinely glad to have us around.

"So what do you like, Miss Emily?" he asks.

"Cheese," she says.

"Cheese, it is." Dad pulls two slices of bread out of the plastic wrapper and hands them to her.

We talk about the Crèches, the warm weather, the close up of Ridge Run. We do not mention Bell or Emily's head or how long I might stay. "John says Creech will be back today."

"From the mystery tour?"

"They've got no idea what the trip was about either. I'm sure Creech will fill everybody in when he's ready."

"Mommy, can we go up to the ridge?" Emily asks.

"Not today, munchkin." I think about all the big machines up at the ski area, the unmanned chairlift, the splinters just waiting for a hand to pass over the rail of the base lodge deck.

My dad looks a little sheepish. "I told her we might go. I need to get up there this afternoon."

Emily waits for me to change my answer. "You need to take a nap," I say. "You have to rest your noggin."

"What's a noggin?" she asks.

"Your head." I pull her onto my lap and tap gently at the bandage. "You need to rest to get better."

Emily squirms. "I rested and rested, Mom. I want to go with Gramps."

"She'll be fine, Mallo. You used to go up there all the time when you were her age. I'll keep a good eye on her. Don't you worry."

But I am worried. My father's reminder that I'd gone up there a lot as a kid doesn't help. I remember how Creech and I, and sometimes Adam and Eric, would jump from the deck rails and swing around on the chairlift seats. One time, we played commando, a game where you had to climb hand over hand on the chairlift cable to the next chair. It's a wonder I never fell on my head.

"I don't know," I say.

"Tell you what," my dad says to Em. "You go rest on the couch for a little while, and I'll talk to your mother here."

Emily looks at me like I'm the big bad wolf. I'm beginning to understand how my own mother must have felt. But she goes off, Coot trailing behind her, and plops down on the couch.

"I wish you hadn't promised her."

"One thing I've learned, honey, is that you

241

can't hang on too hard."

"I'm not hanging on too hard. She's just out of the hospital. She could get hurt."

"I'm not going to let anything happen to her. Any more than I'd let anything happen to you." My dad puts both his hands on my shoulders. "I know you worry after her. Believe me, you always will. But sometimes it's best to let go, just a little."

I get the feeling that we're not talking about Emily anymore.

I watch them from the front window, my dad in his plaid jacket and Olin cap, my little girl skipping along next to him, a sling around her arm and a white bandage sticking out from under her own cap. Her jacket is unzipped and it flies behind her like a pair of wings each time a breeze stirs up. They'd invited me to come along, and I had been sorely tempted to go. In the end I decided against it. My anxiety would hang over the two of them like a fog.

My dad is right, though I am reluctant to admit it. I do need to let go just a little. Still, I watch them go with the tiniest of tremors and find myself mumbling a little prayer for their safety.

I decide to use their absence to treat myself to a long, hot shower. I'd taken a brief one last night, after Emily and my dad both went to bed. I had forgotten how small my dad's water tank is, until ice water sprayed out after a few minutes of bliss. The tank has had hours to refill, stoked by short blasts of hand and dish washing, and I'm ready to bask in the warmth of the first genuine shower in over a week.

I no sooner step into the bathtub, about to

turn on all that magnificent hot water, when I hear a car pull into the drive and a car door slam. The driveway is just under the bathroom's narrow window. Reluctantly, I grab a towel and peek out at whoever it is disturbing my moment. There's Creech's old truck, and Creech ambling towards the door. I curse him a few times, throw my clothes back on, and get to the door before he has a chance to knock on it.

"You spying on me?" he asks. His smile is as broad as the day is sunny and warm.

"I was ready to have a really glorious shower. Until you came by and spoiled it."

He ignores my shower remark. "Where's your dad and the munchkin?"

"They went up to the ridge. I'm here all by my lonely."

"That's good," he says. "Because I wanted to talk to you."

I invite him in and before we have a chance to sit, he says, "I've been offered a job." He shifts foot to foot in a nervous dance, the way he always does when he's got big news.

"You already have a job," I say.

He grabs my shoulders. I'm still a little annoyed with him, but the excitement in his voice is catching.

"They want to make me assistant coach of the women's team," he says.

"The women's team?"

This is big. Until now, Creech has been coaching girls. This is *the* team. These are the girls who have made it, who are competing internationally.

"The big girls, Mallo." He lets out a little war whoop. "Can you believe it?"

We're both jumping up and down.

"Creechie, that's great. That's so great!"

He hugs me hard, then picks me up and swings me around.

"You're the first one I've told," he says. He's got this funny smile, his dimple is pushed in. There's something in his eyes though. Something he's not telling me.

I put my forehead to his. "That's great," I say again.

He pushes me back. "There's only one thing," he says. "The job's based in Park City."

"Utah?" I say as though I've forgotten where Park City is.

"Yeah. If I take it, I'll have to move out there."

"Utah," I repeat.

"I'd start with summer camp in Chile. In June." I nod like this all makes perfect sense. Utah might as well be on the other side of the moon. I'm having a hard time placing Creech in Utah.

Creech puts his hands back on my shoulders. "Say something."

I realize I've been quiet for a while, trying to take the news in.

"It's terrific, Creech," I say. "If anybody deserves it, it's you." There's a knot in my throat, and it's coming out in my voice. I am happy for him. I want him to go. But he's always been there. Always. I can't imagine not having Creech down the road.

He looks at me in a way he hasn't since he went off to ski the circuit after high school, like he wants to make me happy but doesn't know how. "What's wrong?"

"Nothing. I'm emotional these days, is all. And I'm going to miss having you around."

244

"We have phones and airplanes. Nothing's that far."

"You're right. And now I've got an excuse to visit Utah." I change the subject, because his leaving has made me feel vulnerable. "Dad took the munchkin up to the hill. I was thinking about all those things we used to do. Remember when you raced me to the top of the patrol hut roof?"

"We used to sit up there all the time. Nice view." He shakes his head.

"Should I worry?"

"Nah. We're still here. Despite the odds. How is she doing?"

"Better. Rest is a word she doesn't want to hear. I guess that's a good sign." I nod at him and for the first time I don't know what to say. "Hey, you want some coffee? I was going to make a fresh pot."

"No thanks. I should really get going."

He nods too, as though we are polite neighbors, acquaintances instead of lifelong friends. I try to let the feeling go, but I can't. It'll take time to adjust to life without the constant of Creech in it.

Chapter Twenty Eight

That evening I tell my Dad about Creech's new job and he takes it in thoughtfully, saying, as I did, that it's a great opportunity. We watch TV for a while. Despite all the sleep I'm still wrung out, and I go to bed with Emily at eight.

I get up bright and early the next morning and finally get the extra-long, extra-hot shower I've been craving. When I come back to the bedroom, Emily's cot is empty. There's a lot of clanging from downstairs. I dress and go down to find my dad and my daughter in the kitchen. Emily looks as though she's dunked herself in flour. Her pink shirt is nearly as white as the cast on her arm. She uses her good arm to run a wooden spoon around a big ceramic bowl. There are eggshells littering the counter, along with splotches of batter that must have jumped out of the bowl.

"Morning, sweetie." My dad kisses my cheek.

"What's all this?" I ask.

"Pancakes," says Emily.

My father has the griddle out, and he's standing over it with a tub of margarine in hand. He's never, as far as I know, cooked anything more complicated than a hamburger.

I elbow him in the ribs. "Since when do you make pancakes?"

"Got to start some time," he says. "Now get on out of here. Too many cooks make a mess."

I survey the kitchen. "You sure don't need any help in that department." He shoos me away and I grab a cup of coffee and skeedaddle.

I take the coffee out to the porch. It's another near perfect day, warm enough to go out without a jacket. I look out towards the mountain and wonder what Bell is doing this minute. I can't help wishing he would call, though I know he won't. I asked for time and space, and he will give it to me, give me acres of it, more time and space than I need.

The pancakes are burnt on one side and have the texture of rubber cement. We eat them anyway. Even Emily eats them. And we declare them delicious.

After we clean up the mess, Emily and I take Coot out for a walk. We go to the pond, the place Creech and I used to skinny dip as teenagers. The postage-stamp beach is clear of snow, though there is still a thin skin of ice where the water is shaded by pines. I pick up some flat stones and show Emily how to skim them. She uses her good arm, her right, to toss them. They plunk into the water without skipping. On the seventh or eighth try, she finally gets one to bounce and it lands on the ice and skids along for quite a distance.

Emily jumps up and down. "Did you see that, Mom?" she says. "Did you see?"

I put my arm around her and give her a squeeze. "You're going to be a champion stone skipper someday." And I believe, without a doubt, she will be, maybe not a champion stone skipper, but a champion nonetheless.

We pass the Crèche home on the way back from the pond. The house started out as a regular Cape Cod, but has since had so many rooms added on that it looks like a telescope with a wide middle. On the way back, we catch Creech's dad, John, pulling out of the driveway in his truck. He stops halfway down the drive and jumps from the cab. He gives me a hug and twirls Emily around in a big circle.

"Your dad's one lucky man, having two pretty girls around," he says.

We talk for a bit about the warm weather and the last weeks on the hill. Emily soon gets bored with the conversation and begins chasing Coot across the lawn.

"Great news about Creech," I say.

"Sure is," says John.

"He here?"

"No, actually, he went out to hike the ridge a little while back."

"Alone?" It isn't like Creech to do anything alone. Though I suppose with neither of his brothers around he might not have found anyone to drag along. I'm a little hurt he didn't ask me, but then again, maybe he stopped by after Em and I had already left.

"Marie's inside. Said she was going to bake some cookies to bring down to you. She'd love it if you pop in."

I agree we will and John hops back into the truck.

"Mallo?" he says before shutting the door, "Creech say anything else to you? About the job?'

"Not really. He told me it's a big promotion and it's in Park City. He must have told you the same thing."

"Yes, I suppose he did." John sweeps the concern from his face with a smile, but I catch it anyway.

The Crèche house smells, as it always has, of a terrific mix of baking cookies, mud, and pine cleaner. Marie is all smiles when we walk in the door. She's a little thicker around the waist than she used to be, but she looks almost exactly the way she did when I was growing up—small-boned, blond, with the hazel eyes all three of her boys inherited. She soon has me sitting at the kitchen table while she shows Emily how to stir chips into a batch of chocolate chip cookies. She pours me some coffee without my asking from the pot that's always going in her kitchen, then puts some milk on the stove so that she can make Emily some hot chocolate to go with the cookies.

It's warm and cozy in here. Coot has settled under the kitchen table with a satisfied snort. We chat as though I've lived my whole life down the road with my dad and never left for college or Albany or Lake Placid. She mentions that Eric's coming home for good in a few weeks and you can see how pleased she is with this. "It's great having the boys back," she says. "Though with Creech, it's only for a little bit." She refills my coffee cup and shows Emily how to drop dough by the teaspoonful onto the baking sheet. "You just missed him," she says.

"John said he went up to the ridge."

Marie nods, her brows knit together for a minute as she helps Emily with the spoon. "Went off without saying much this morning."

This, too, is unusual. Creech is not usually at a loss for words. "What's up with him, do you suppose?'

She looks up at me a minute. "I thought you might know."

But I don't know. I haven't the foggiest.

When the cookies are done, Emily downs three right from the oven and would have eaten more, if I hadn't stopped her with a warning about a tummy ache.

"You can take them with you for later," Marie says, wrapping the plate. She hands the plate to me "It's hard being a good mom sometimes."

Emily wanders off to the dining room. Marie keeps a tin of spare buttons in the hutch and Emily remembers them from her last visit. She asks Marie if she can play with them. Marie gets the button tin out for her and soon Emily's absorbed with laying multi-colored buttons out on the dining room table.

"Sometimes I wonder if I am a good mother," I say as we watch Emily sort.

Marie is a good mother. She's the best. For years I harbored a secret wish that she were my mother. Of course, I felt guilty every time I wished it, because my own mother did love me. But how much easier it would have been growing up at the Crèche's. Then again, I practically did grow up at the Crèche's.

Emily starts putting buttons together into a mosaic of some kind. She sings, "Number one, number one, now the song has just begun." Bell taught her that song. Last summer. Emily was already learning to count and she spent the better part of the plane ride to New Zealand practicing that song. She sang it for Roddie and Sue when we got to Craigeborne.

Marie's hand comes up and squeezes my shoulder. "You are a good mother, Mallo," she says. "Don't you ever believe otherwise."

Tears spring to my eyes. Good mothers don't let their little girls fall from trees. Good mothers don't make their little girl's daddies lie to them. The tears run down my cheeks and then Marie catches me up in her arms. She's a few inches shorter than me. Small, just like my real mother.

"It's okay," she says. "It's okay." She steers me towards the kitchen door. "Come on. Let me show you my new azalea bush."

I look back towards Em.

Marie turns the door knob and swings open the back door. "She'll be just fine"

"I worry about her so much," I say when we get outside.

"She's fine, Mallo. Accidents happen sometimes. Look at the boys."

I wonder if she's thinking about Creech, that terrible month he spent in a Swiss hospital after his fall at Grindlewald. He went right back to racing as soon as he was able. I never wondered before about how that must have been for Marie.

"My dad says I'm holding on too tight."

"Of course, you are. It wouldn't be natural for you not to. But sooner or later, you got to let go a little," she says, repeating my father's words.

We stand on the muddy side lawn gazing at a spindly bush that hasn't begun to leaf out yet. "John put it in for me last week. I think it will flower this spring."

I nod dumbly. I'm not up to talking about azalea bushes.

Marie takes my hand. "I almost left John once or twice early on," she says. "Back when we were young, before we settled in here and had the boys. Your Bell reminds me of him. He liked to go off and have adventures. The more dangerous the better. I used to worry after him something fierce. Didn't think I could hold on."

"You did, though."

"Sure I did." She gives me a long look. "Sometimes, you know how it's supposed to be. John always came home to me. I never once

251

doubted he loved me." Then she smiles at me. "I always thought you'd end up with Creech, the way you two were when you were kids."

"It'd be nice to be part of this family."

"Honey, you are part of this family. No matter what happens, you'll always be part of this family."

The tears, which had taken a momentary leave, prick at my eyes again. "I don't know what to do, Marie."

"You just follow your heart, Mallo. It hasn't steered you wrong yet."

Chapter Twenty Nine

I keep looking out towards the ridge all the way back to my dad's house, enough so that Emily asks me why. I tell her it's because I spent a lot of time up there when I was a little girl like her. She's satisfied with this answer, but it's not the truth. The truth is I'm hoping to catch a glimpse of Creech. It bothers me that he's gone off alone, enough so that when Em and I get back to my dad's I tell him that I'm going to go for a walk. He looks at me a little funny, because I've just been for a walk, but pretty soon he and Emily are sitting down to an intense game of Old Maid and I'm all but forgotten.

I think I know where Creech is. There's a ledge along the backside of the mountain. Few people know it's there. We used to go there to be alone when we were teenagers. I take the ridge trail, the steepest and most direct of the ski trails, to get to the top. I'm soon sorry over my choice. Dry weeds thwack into my knees. The ground is still splattered with snow and soggy where the snow has melted. There's a lake-size puddle near the base of the trail that's hard to skirt, and I manage to stick my boot ankle deep into the mire.

It takes me half an hour to make the climb. From here, there is an old access road and a narrow trail that leads off to the ledge. The road and trail are on the north side of the mountain and the snow is knee-deep in spots. It takes me twenty minutes to pick my way down to the ledge. By the time I get there, I'm pretty sure Creech has already left, if he was ever there at all.

Sure enough, at first glance he's not there. I curse out loud and then I spy him, sitting under some large rocks at the far side. He turns when he hears me but he does not get up. The sun has warmed the ledge. It's snow-free and dry, and I find it easy to make my way over to him.

Far below us, the Sacandaga River snakes between the mountains, the water already swollen with winter runoff. All around the round hills of the southern Adirondack range ebb and flow, waves of pine and rock and trees bare of leaves.

"I've forgotten how pretty this is," I say.

He's looking out at the scenery, his arms around his knees. He doesn't answer me.

"What's with you?" I say.

"Nothing, Mallo. I came up here to be alone for a while."

"Since when do you go anywhere alone?"

He turns to give me a long hard look and then goes back to contemplating the landscape.

The silence is more than I can stand. "Is this about the job?" I ask, not willing to let it go like he wants me to.

He still doesn't answer.

"Are you having second thoughts?"

"Opportunity of a lifetime," he says.

"It is. You should be thrilled."

"I am thrilled, Mallo. Why wouldn't I be?" He picks up a stone, fingers it, and throws it down over the ledge. It bounces and shoots into the saplings.

"So you're going to take it."

"Yes. I am. Why wouldn't I?" He gets up and walks to the pine growing out of the rocks, puts both hands to the trunk, and leans in. "I think I'm going to like Utah. Mountains, powder, what's not

254

to like?"

"I'm going to miss you something awful. I know, I know, phones and planes. But it won't be the same, will it?"

He comes back over to me and cups his hand under my chin. "I'm going to miss you, too." He kisses my forehead. I put my arms around him. Once upon a time, this would have led to us pulling each other down to the ground and shedding some clothes, but this isn't once upon a time anymore.

When he looks at me, his eyes are wet. My own eyes have filled. "I love you, you know," I say.

"I love you too, Mallo Cup." He shakes his head and laughs sadly. "Sometimes I wish we were still sixteen. I had it all figured out back then."

"I wish it, too, sometimes." If I'd loved Creech more, or differently, maybe we wouldn't be standing here like this.

"Things are what they are." Creech smooths his hand over my hair. "I had this crazy idea you could come with me, and we'd live happily ever after in Park City."

"Creech—"

"It's a fantasy. I know that. We aren't sixteen anymore. I had to let go of you a long time ago, Mallo. You've got another man. A kid."

The words break my heart. The world has gone liquid. The hills and trees beyond the ledge float away. From here, we can see both of our houses, the ones we grew up in, dotting the road. They seem so small, too small to have contained us. Too small to have contained our lives, which is may be why we left them in the first place. And which, I suppose, is why neither of us will be able to stay here for long.

"I really do love you," I repeat.

"That's what makes leaving so frigging hard."

Chapter Thirty

I feel that I should run all the way back to my dad's. That somehow I can outrun this feeling, the one I can't quite name, the one I want to leave behind on the ridge with Creech. And I start back. My boots dislodge loose rocks on the way down the trail and strike heavily on the gravel road. I turn and jog back up towards the ridge, then down again detouring the long way around the pond to get back to my father's house. I force myself to go fast enough to make my heart pound, proof it's still right where I left it, untattered.

I don't slow until I get to my dad's driveway, and then I stop short. Bell's Jeep is parked in the drive.

I walk the distance to the house, breathing in fiercely to recapture the air. My mind is spread like the mud along the banks of the Sacandaga, running out in five directions at once. Inside the house, I find my dad curled up in his recliner, flipping through channels with the remote. He is alone. My eyes ask questions.

"You just missed them," he says. "They went up to find you."

"I came down the road. Didn't see anyone."

"Must be up on the hill then."

For a minute or two I don't know what to do. Half of me wants to race back up the road and the other half wants to stay here, to take the time Bell promised me. I'm already sure there is no staying put though. Not for any of us. So I keep my coat on and head back out the door. I walk this time. Each step is a decision I keep making. Over and over I make the same decision. I walk towards them.

I see them from the foot of the ridge trail. They are on their way up, a lanky blond man with a little blonde girl on his shoulders, a dog at their side.

It's Chance who discovers me first. He comes racing down the trail, bounding over rocks and snow and shallow spring melt. He dances around me and muddies me with his wet paws and licks my hand. The two of us wait while Bell and Emily pick their way back down to us. Emily's got a smile the size of the sun. Bell's not smiling—he's eyeing me, unsure.

"Mommy, we found you!" says my little girl when Bell puts her down. "Daddy brought Chancie!"

Bell puts Chance on the leash, and the dog pulls him back towards my father's house. We start walking down the road. Bell and I walk side by side. His steps seem as tentative as mine.

"Chance looks good," I say.

"Danny took good care of him. Just before I got him back, I bought one of those invisible fences we were talking about. That should keep him corralled."

I wonder if a fence is what I need or what I want. Bell has never liked fences. Emily grabs his other hand and skips along between us. From a distance, we must look like the perfect family. Though here between us the distance is gone and appearances are deceiving.

We let Emily go inside with Chance and the two of us stand in the driveway, facing each other. We haven't said much and I don't know how to start it, this conversation. I don't know where it will end.

Bell begins it. "I know I said I'd give you time." He looks at me long, as though he were trying to memorize me. I have to look away. I look up to the mountain; notice the sun dancing off wet rocks, the trees still along the grassy edges of the slope. I feel his hands on my shoulders, the gravity of them enough to squeeze tears.

"I was home. Only it wasn't home," he says. "It's not home without you and Emily there."

I manage to look now. His blue eyes catch me, and I almost close mine against them.

"I want so much to make it right." The clouds snag on my dad's rooftop. "But after I saw you in the hospital—that look in your eyes—I put that look in your eyes. I don't think I'll ever forgive myself for that." He draws a ragged breath. "So if you can't come back, I'll have to live with that. I'll have to let you go. But, God, I don't want to."

He runs his hands along my shoulders and I take one of them. His fingers are long and smooth, the nails chewed down with the restlessness he holds. I want to believe him, but the only thought in my mind is how long until the next Denali?

"I don't know what to do," I tell him. "I've been so scared, you going up there on the West Rib. I know you're good. I know you're the best, but up there, who knows what will happen. I get so scared of losing you."

He pulls me in. He smells of wood and moist spring air.

"Up there, coming down, it was you I thought about. You and Emily and coming home. That was all I wanted up there. To be with you and Emily. In the end, that's the only thing really counts for anything at all. I don't tell you. Maybe I should. But that's the truth of it, Mallo. You and Emily count for everything."

He lets go, steps back and shoves his hands into his pockets. The sun has already begun to move down through the trees. It dapples everything: Bell's shoulders, his Adam's apple, the curve of his arm inside the fleece jacket he wears. I feel as dappled as the late afternoon light, my shadow fluttering in pieces.

I know how hard the words are for him. After seven years, I know how much it has cost him to come here and speak them.

"I need you to know I love you," he says. "I'll give you time. I'll go home and I won't ask you to come with me. But, God Mallo, I'd trade everything I own for another chance with you."

I stand in the door when he hugs Emily goodbye. He promises he'll see her soon and then closes his eyes and takes her in. Emily and I watch as he drives off with Chance, the pair of us drooped together on the front porch.

Later that evening, my mom calls as we're doing the supper dishes. She asks after Emily and I put her on the phone. After Emily's done talking my dad gets on the phone and he and mom talk for a long time. He comes back to drying with the slightest smile on his lips and tells me that next time we go to Albany, he'd like to come along.

We watch TV, though none of the program sinks in. My mind is far away, thinking about Bell. I keep picturing him at the cabin sitting alone on the porch with Chance. There's a terrible homesickness in the picture. There's a piece missing.

Emily puts voice to it when I tuck her onto the

cot. "Mommy," she says. "I'm ready to go home now."

I kiss her goodnight and climb onto my old bed. I watch her for a long time, her blonde hair curling over the pillow. She reminds me so much of Bell.

Unable to sleep, I slip downstairs in the dark and go out on the porch. I'm barefoot and the boards are frosted. There's a full moon hanging low over the ridge. Out from somewhere, a catamount lets out a plaintive cry, sounding like a child lost in the woods. I've never been lost in these woods, and I'm no child. I'm a full-grown woman with a child. And north of here, there is a man who loves me and awaits my return.

I stand there long enough for the tips of my fingers to feel the freeze. My breath comes in even clouds. I've had enough time.

By the time Emily wakes in the morning I've got our few things packed. I've made coffee and I'm working on eggs and bacon. My dad stands in the kitchen door. "You've made a decision," he says.

"Can't stay and mooch off my old man forever," I tell him. "May I borrow your truck?"

He laughs. "Sure. Just get it back to me in one piece, okay?"

I call Emily and we sit to breakfast.

"You're doing the right thing," my dad says.

"I hope so."

"No," he says. "You know it as well as I."

He's right. I do know. I've known all along. There are some things I can't leave behind, not even if I try.

"Get dressed," I tell Em after breakfast. "We're going home."

Chapter Thirty One

We wind our way up Route 30, past a hundred familiar sights. The early morning mountains are dappled in fog that rises from snowmelt. We name the lakes with ice biting their edges as we pass—Pleasant, Louie, Indian, Blue Mountain, Long, Saranac. Each one is a step closer to home.

It's late morning by the time we curl through Lake Placid's Main Street. Tourists stroll by the shops that line Mirror Lake. The lake itself is a silver wafer. We drive down past the ice rink, towards where the Intervale ski jump tower rises, an unlikely skyscraper capping the trees. I turn down our road, rutted deeper than it was when we'd left it. The peaks brood around us. Snow drips into gullies, pines nestle familiar along the sidelines. I pull into the drive feeling as though I've been away for years, and the journey has brought me back to where I began. Smoke rises from the chimney of the cabin, clouds dissipating in the crystalline sky.

Chance barks and Emily scrambles from the car seat to meet him, a head-on collision of little girl and dog. I'm slower in getting out. I want to take it all in: the hemlocks tossing in the light breeze, Tawahus splitting the sky, wood smoke clinging to the air, mud sucking at my boots. Bell stands in the open bay of the garage. The smell of woodchips is pungent. He puts down his sander and Emily runs to him. I walk closer and he watches me as he scoops our daughter into his arms, his eyes bright.

We look at each other for a forever of moments. Emily shifts in Bell's arms, Chance sniffs back and forth between us. Emily finally lets go of Bell and asks if she can take Chance into the yard. Bell tells her sure, and she walks away, the dog trotting beside her, looking over her shoulder, already older at four than the two of us.

"What's this?" I ask, nodding towards the wood that Bell was working when we drove in.

"Maple branches," he says, smoothing his careful hand over the planed wood. "I'm not sure. Table, maybe."

Maple branches.

He catches my look and seems to stutter over it for a minute. "I cut the lower ones off that tree. Should have done it a long time ago." He looks at the wood as though it had betrayed him. "I never thought...."

"It was an accident," I say. And for the first time I see it that way. There is no one to blame. Not Bell, not me. What happened simply happened.

He touches the wood again. "I wanted to be here," he says. "You've got to believe that."

I step close to him. "I know."

I do know. What he told me that last day in the hospital is true. This is the place he belongs. The place we both belong.

I trace the line of his jaw with my fingers. "We should get married," I say, echoing his long ago words. I hope he knows I mean it.

He cups his hand over mine and raises it to his lips. He kisses my palm. I circle my other arm around his waist. His jacket smells of pine boughs and spring air, the smell of home. We dance together, stepping and swaying in a tethered circle.

I hold on the way I need to, knowing I won't let

go.

About Ute

Ute Carbone is the author of 9 novels, 4 novellas, and a short story collection. Her books include SWEET AURALIE, which, was awarded an EPIC for best historical novel and the novella ALL THINGS RETURNED, which was voted best Civil War Era historical romance by Hearts through History, the historical arm of RWA. When not writing or reading one of the many books on her to be read list, Ute enjoys walking in the woods, feeding her photography habit, and drinking more cups of coffee than she should.

www.ingramcontent.com/pod-product-compliance
Lightning Source LLC
Chambersburg PA
CBHW011459170626
46814CB00008B/2960